W9-CBM-037

MANDIE®

AND JONATHAN'S PREDICAMENT

Lois Gladys Leppard

BETHANY HOUSE PUBLISHERS
MINNEAPOLIS, MINNESOTA 55438

This book is especially for

MARY LINDSEY,

who has lived a life just like Mandie's,
and who has grown up reading about Mandie,
and who is now in college,
with love and gratitude.

About the Author

LOIS GLADYS LEPPARD worked in Federal Intelligence for thirteen years in various countries around the world. She now makes her home in South Carolina.

The stories of her mother's childhood as an orphan in Western North Carolina are the basis for many of the incidents incorporated in this series.

Visit her Web site: www.Mandie.com

Contents

"Lives of great men all remind us
We can make our lives sublime,
And, departing, leave behind us
Footprints on the sands of time."

—from "A Psalm of Life"
Henry Wadsworth Longfellow
(1807–1882)

Chapter 1 / New York at Last!

Mandie gasped as she stepped outside the noisy train depot in New York. She looked around in disbelief at what seemed like hundreds of people rushing in every direction.

"Where are all the people going?" Mandie asked. Snowball, her white cat, clung to the shoulder of her coat as she stopped to stare.

At that instant a tall man carrying a huge bag on his shoulder swiped by her, almost pushing off her wool tam. She snatched at her hat and managed to get it back in place with one hand.

"Come on, girls," Jane Hamilton said, giving her daughter, Celia, a slight push forward through the crowd. Looking back, she added, "Amanda, if you just stand there, the people will literally run over top of you."

Mandie quickly walked on with her friend Celia Hamilton.

"Sorry, we forgot to warn you about the people

here being in such a fizz," Celia said with a big smile. She dipped her head to dodge an open umbrella a woman was carrying, even though it was not raining.

Mandie tried to see where they were going, but the crowd blocked her view. She looked upward and gasped again at the sight of several monstrous buildings nearby. Pedestrians shoved against her as they rushed past, and she had to hurry to keep up with Celia.

Celia's mother was directing their baggage into a carriage on the street.

"The Waldorf-Astoria Hotel," Mrs. Hamilton told the driver. She motioned for the girls to enter the vehicle, then she followed.

"The Waldorf-Astoria it be, missus," the short, chubby driver said as he closed the door behind them and then jumped up on his seat.

Mandie clutched Snowball and tried to see the city through the carriage window as the driver raced the horses at breakneck speed up the avenue. She held her breath as she saw people risking their lives by dashing across the street between motorcars and horsedrawn vehicles that were moving rapidly in both directions. Most of the people were bundled up in thick coats and warm hats in the cold November weather, so Mandie thought to herself that if they were struck they would at least have a lot of padding on them.

"It's exciting to be in New York, isn't it?" Celia remarked as she turned to look at Mandie from the other side of the carriage, where she had also been gazing out the window.

"Yes, but the people sure are in a hurry," Mandie replied without taking her gaze away from the street. "They act like they're all rushing off to some mysterious place." Then quickly turning to look at her friend, she said, "I imagine New York is full of mysteries." She paused to grin and then added, "Maybe we can find one to solve while we're here."

Mrs. Hamilton, sitting on the opposite seat, smiled at Mandie and said, "I don't think we'll have time to go looking for mysteries."

"Well then, maybe we'll just happen to run into one," Mandie told her with a smile.

"Mandie, I hope not," Celia said. "We've got so many things planned to do, and we are only going to be here this week because we have to go back to school next week, remember."

"I know," Mandie said with a slight groan.

The carriage came to a sudden halt, and Mandie looked outside. They had stopped in front of a building so tall she couldn't see the top.

The carriage door opened and the driver announced, "The Waldorf-Astoria Hotel, missus."

Mrs. Hamilton led the way out of the vehicle, and the girls followed.

"You mean we are going to stay in this huge building?" Mandie questioned in disbelief as she still tried to see the top from where she stood clutching Snowball.

"Yes, this is the Waldorf-Astoria Hotel," Mrs. Hamilton told her as the driver began unloading their baggage. "It has one thousand rooms and is the largest hotel in the world."

"One thousand rooms!" Mandie exclaimed as she and Celia followed Mrs. Hamilton into the building. "How will we ever find our way around?"

Mrs. Hamilton looked at her and smiled as she said, "Don't worry about that. We'll manage. I've been here before." She went to the desk in the lobby to check in.

A hotel employee in a neat red uniform with lots of braid on it took them and their baggage up to their rooms on the fifth floor. Mandie's stomach almost turned over when they stepped inside the elevator and it began moving upward. She held her breath until the thing stopped and the man opened the door. Rushing out into the hallway, she exhaled and held tightly to Snowball.

"Oh!" she exclaimed to herself.

"I didn't like the ride, either," Celia confided as the two girls followed Mrs. Hamilton and the man down the long hallway to their rooms.

Once they were inside one of the rooms, Mrs. Hamilton said, "You girls will share this room, and I will be right next door." She directed the man with the luggage. He left the girls' things in that room, then Mrs. Hamilton showed him where to take hers.

The girls followed her through a bathroom and into another bedroom.

"Everything is so fine," Mandie remarked, looking at the furniture and draperies.

The man left, and as soon as the door closed behind him, Mrs. Hamilton said, "I had already asked for a sandbox for your cat, Amanda, so you should go see if there's one in your room. I do hope Snowball won't damage anything. And, girls, get your dresses out of your trunks and freshen up after that long train ride. As soon as y'all change your clothes, we'll go down to the dining room and find something to eat."

"Yes, ma'am," Mandie replied.

"We'll hurry, Mother," Celia promised, " 'cause I'm awfully hungry."

As the girls rushed back into their room, Mandie said, "You know, I don't believe any of those hotels we stayed in last summer in Europe were this big or this nice." She saw a sandbox in a corner and set her cat in it.

"I know," Celia agreed as she opened her trunk. "But then Mother just said this is the largest hotel in the world."

Mandie went over to her trunk and opened it. "I wish Grandmother could have come with us," she said, taking out a dress and shaking it. "But for some reason she didn't want me to come, much less her."

Celia straightened up as she unpacked and said, "I think there's something wrong somewhere, somehow, between Jonathan's father and your grandmother. She never wants to associate with the man, and she knew very well that if we came to New York we would certainly go visit Jonathan."

"I agree," Mandie said, pausing to look at her friend. "I've been puzzled about that, and I can't figure out what it's all about."

"Maybe Jonathan knows. We can ask him," Celia said as she slipped off her brown traveling suit and hung it up in the huge wardrobe.

Mandie removed her navy suit and hung it next to Celia's. "Has your mother decided when we'll go to see Jonathan and his father?" she asked.

"No, all she has said is that we will visit them," Celia said.

"I want to see Dr. Plumbley, too," Mandie told her as they continued hanging up their clothes. "He will be surprised to see us all the way up here in New York."

"I hope you brought his address," Celia said.

"I have it in my purse," Mandie replied, picking up the small drawstring bag she had laid on the bed.

"Do you think Jonathan's father will invite us to have Thanksgiving dinner with them Thursday?" Celia asked as she took clean stockings from her trunk.

"I hope so," Mandie said. "But we'll have to let him know we're here pretty soon so he can have time to get the meal prepared if we're going."

"Well, today's just Monday. I'm sure he has plenty of servants to cook and all that," Celia told her.

Mrs. Hamilton called through the closed door to the bathroom, "Hurry up, girls. I'm finished in here now."

"Yes, Mother," Celia replied.

A few minutes later the three of them went back downstairs. Mandie left Snowball shut up in the bathroom, and Mrs. Hamilton led the way to the dining room. A man in uniform standing by the door took Jane's name and led them to a table by a window that was partially obscured by tall potted plants.

Mandie looked around as she sat down in the plush-seated chair. Lots of well-dressed people were seated throughout the room, and the fragrance of the food made her realize she was about to starve. She was delighted to find the hotel had fried chicken on the menu. She had been secretly afraid that the food in New York would be something strange.

After they had all ordered and while they waited for the waiter to return with their food, Mrs. Hamilton told them her plans. "As soon as we eat, I'll call Jonathan's house and you girls can decide when you want to get together with him," she said.

"Call?" Mandie questioned. And then she quickly added, "Oh, of course, there are telephones in this hotel, aren't there?"

"Yes, quite a few, and I imagine Jonathan's father has a telephone in his house. You see, this city is so far ahead of everything back home," Mrs. Hamilton replied.

"But we have telephones in Franklin," Mandie said. "And Grandmother says she's going to have a telephone installed in the school where Celia and I go and also in her house. Then she won't have to ride over to the school so much. She'll be able to talk to Miss Prudence and Miss Hope on the telephone."

"They have telephones in Richmond, too," Mrs. Hamilton replied. "But we're so far out in the country, we'll have to wait for them to run the lines out there from Richmond. I do hope it will be soon. Telephones are a great convenience, just like motorcars are becoming."

"Do you think we might buy a motorcar some day, Mother?" Celia asked.

"Yes, one day, when they've improved the roads. Right now there are not enough roadways to make a motorcar worthwhile," Celia's mother told her. "Not only that, your aunt Rebecca and I would have to learn to steer the thing, and someone would have to know what to do if it quit going."

"In other words, it would be an enormous undertaking to own one," Mandie remarked. "I like carriages better. They're not so complicated."

"Yes, just feed and take care of the horses, hitch up the carriage any time you get ready, and drive down all those muddy, bumpy roads we have back home," Celia agreed with a laugh.

"Now here's our food," Mrs. Hamilton said as the waiter rolled a cart holding trays of steaming meats and vegetables up to their table. "Let's make short work of this meal so we can use the telephone."

Mandie and Celia were both hungry and anxious to contact Jonathan, so they devoured their food. In no time at all, they were following Mrs. Hamilton to a telephone on a small table in the lobby of the hotel. She picked it up, putting the tall piece to her mouth and the cylinder attached on a cord to her ear.

"Number please," the girls could plainly hear a voice coming over the telephone.

"I don't have the number, but would you please ring Mr. Lindall Guyer, that is, Mr. Jonathan Lindall Guyer, the second? He lives on Fifth Avenue," Mrs. Hamilton explained.

"Thank you," the voice came over the telephone again, then a loud buzzing noise was heard.

Suddenly another voice sounded on the telephone. "This is Mr. Guyer's residence," a man said with a British accent.

"Is Mr. Guyer at home, please? This is Mrs. Hamilton from Richmond, Virginia, and I am calling from the Waldorf-Astoria Hotel," Jane told him.

"He is not here at the moment, mum, but he should be returning soon. I will give him your name," the man said.

"Also, please give him my daughter's name, Celia, and her friend Amanda Shaw, who are with me. Thank you," she replied.

"Righto, mum, that I will," the man said and broke the connection.

Mrs. Hamilton hung up the phone and looked at the two girls. "Maybe Mr. Guyer will telephone us when he returns home," she said as she walked toward a sofa on the other side of the lobby.

"I hope so," Celia said.

"So that's all you do to call up someone else's telephone," Mandie remarked as she and Celia followed Mrs. Hamilton to the sofa where they all sat down.

"It's not hard at all, and think of the time it saves when you want to get in touch with someone," Mrs. Hamilton said.

"Provided the person you want to talk to has a telephone," Celia added.

"I think maybe the telephone is a good idea," Mandie said, smiling. "When Grandmother gets hers, I'll ask Mother to get one. Then I won't have to go all the way home from school in Asheville to talk to her."

"Yes, and maybe Mr. Chadwick's School will get one, too, and we can call the boys over there," Celia said with a big grin.

"And maybe Joe Woodard's father will get one, too. After all, he's a doctor and should have one," Mandie added thoughtfully. "I just don't know about Uncle Ned. He might not want a telephone."

Uncle Ned was Mandie's father's old Cherokee friend. The year before, Jim Shaw had died and Uncle Ned had promised her father that he would watch over Mandie. He kept his promise and almost always turned up wherever she went.

"Oh, but, dear, you have to have telephone lines to connect your telephone, and I don't imagine there would be any lines way out there in Deep

Creek where Uncle Ned lives," Mrs. Hamilton explained.

"Well, he probably wouldn't get one anyway," Mandie decided.

They got into a deep conversation about telephones and time flew by. Suddenly Mandie was startled to see Jonathan Guyer and his father coming toward them across the lobby. She quickly grabbed Celia's hand.

"Celia, here comes Jonathan!" she cried, excitedly jumping up from the sofa.

Celia also rose and uttered a loud "Jonathan!"

Jonathan ran ahead of his father and quickly tried to embrace both girls at one time. "Mandie! Celia!" he exclaimed. "You didn't let us know you were coming."

Mandie looked up into his mischievous black eyes and said, "But we did let you know we were here."

"It would have been TB for you if you hadn't," Jonathan replied, squeezing her hand.

"TB? What does that mean?" Mandie asked.

Jonathan looked at her in surprise and said, "Why, it means *too bad*. Oh, I forgot y'all come from down in the country and are probably behind with New York slang." He grinned.

Lindall Guyer approached the sofa, and Jane Hamilton rose.

"My, my, what are you doing in a hotel when I have such a big house? I must insist you check out of here immediately and come home with us," he told Mrs. Hamilton as he squeezed her hand.

She looked up at the smiling man and said, "Oh, but we couldn't impose on you. You see, we have plans for so many things in the short time we'll be here."

"Never mind excuses," Mr. Guyer said. "Seems like I remember you were always making up excuses long years ago when we first met. Now let's get your things. I have my carriage waiting outside."

The three young people had been listening to the conversation. Mandie was aware that her grandmother knew Jonathan's father, and it was evident that Celia's mother did as well. But then when you were as wealthy and well known as Lindall Guyer, it was no surprise that everyone seemed to be acquainted with the man.

"Please, Mother," Celia spoke up.

"Please, Mrs. Hamilton," Jonathan added.

Mrs. Hamilton looked at the dark young man and said, "Jonathan, I am pleased to finally meet you. Celia and Amanda have talked about you so much since they met you on the trip to Europe back in the summer that I feel as though I already know you."

"I'm pleased to meet you, Mrs. Hamilton," Jonathan replied, and then with a big grin he added, "But we could all get better acquainted if you just move on over to our house."

"Yes, let's get someone to bring down your luggage," Mr. Guyer told Mrs. Hamilton as he glanced around the lobby.

"We will have to go up and repack a little first," Mrs. Hamilton replied.

"And get Snowball! Goodness, I almost forgot about him. He hasn't even been fed yet," Mandie told them, suddenly realizing her cat must be awfully hungry by now.

"So you brought that white cat with you," Jonathan teased. "Remember all the trouble he caused on that ship going to England? But he won't be any trouble at our house. We have lots of rooms for him to roam in."

While Mandie and the Hamiltons went to their rooms to repack, Mr. Guyer and Jonathan went outside to get their driver to help the hotel employee bring the luggage down and stack it in the Guyers' huge, rich-looking carriage. Finally they were all on their way to Jonathan's house.

The three young people excitedly reminisced about their adventures on the journey to Europe. Mrs. Hamilton listened to them and smiled. Mr. Guyer smiled as he watched her.

Before anyone realized it, the driver was turning the carriage into the driveway of Lindall Guyer's house.

Chapter 2 / Poor Fellow

Mandie stared at the huge stone building Jonathan called his home as the carriage came to a halt under a portico. The driver jumped down and opened the door, and another man, evidently the butler, came out of the house to assist with their luggage.

"The North Carolina room and the Virginia room, Jens," Lindall Guyer directed the butler with the bags. Turning to Mrs. Hamilton, he said, "Let's get inside. It's cold out here. I heard there is a possibility of snow today."

Mrs. Hamilton went along with him as he led the way into the house. Mandie followed, clutching Snowball, and Celia came behind her with Jonathan. Both the girls looked around in fascination at the luxurious furnishings in the parlor that opened off the corridor from the outside door.

"Let's sit in here and have some coffee while your rooms are being readied," Mr. Guyer told them.

At that moment a maid in a neat uniform

popped into the room and stood attentively waiting for Mr. Guyer to speak.

"Please take the ladies' coats, Monet," he told her.

Jonathan held Snowball while they removed their coats and hats. Mandie realized Mr. Guyer had included her and Celia as "ladies" to the maid. This gave her a grown-up feeling even though she and Celia were only thirteen years old.

"And, Monet, coffee please, in here," Mr. Guyer added as the maid hung the coats and hats on a clothes tree by the hall door.

"And something to eat for Snowball," Jonathan added as he let the cat down on the floor and held the end of Snowball's red leash out to the maid.

Monet quickly stepped back and looked at Mr. Guyer, then at the cat.

"You will need to take him to the kitchen to feed him, Monet," Jonathan told her, still holding out the end of the leash. "Come on. He won't bite you."

Monet stood there without moving. Mandie sensed she was afraid of Snowball. "I could just take him to the kitchen if you'll show me the way," Mandie offered as she looked at the maid.

"No, Monet will take him," Mr. Guyer spoke up. "The cat will be staying here with us this week with our guests, Monet, so you will have to get used to him."

Everyone watched as Monet silently accepted the end of the leash from Jonathan and started toward the door. Snowball decided to run, and Monet had to rush after him. As soon as they were outside the room, everyone laughed.

"I'm sorry, but she's afraid of all pets—cats, dogs, even birds. But we've never owned a pet, and

Monet has been with us ever since Jonathan was born," Mr. Guyer explained. "Please sit and relax. We'll have coffee shortly."

Mrs. Hamilton stepped over to an upholstered chair by the fireplace where a fire was giving out warmth, and Mr. Guyer sat in the chair opposite her. The young people gathered on a settee nearby.

Jonathan brought the girls up to date on how he was doing. He was living at home and attending a private school on the other side of Central Park.

"Even though my father still travels around a lot, I am at home now when he does come back. We have finally got to know each other," he told the girls.

"I remember you telling us about all those boarding schools you were sent off to," Celia said.

"And never getting to really know your father because he was always going off somewhere on business," Mandie added. "I'm so glad things have changed for you."

"He is getting up in age. Maybe he'll retire someday. You know, Mandie, he's as old as your grandmother. My mother was a lot younger, twenty years in fact," Jonathan explained. "And by the way, why didn't your grandmother come with you?"

Mandie and Celia glanced at each other, and Jonathan looked puzzled by their reaction. Before Mandie could answer, he asked, "Did I say something wrong?"

"Oh no, not at all," Mandie quickly replied. "It's just that my grandmother didn't want to come."

"She didn't?" Jonathan asked, not understanding.

"No, you see, she has so many things to do, always looking after her business and everything," Mandie tried to explain, but secretly she was thinking about the fact that her grandmother didn't even want her to visit the Guyers for some odd reason. She couldn't figure out why her grandmother acted like that every time Lindall Guyer's name was mentioned.

"Well, at least she allowed you to come," Jonathan said.

"My mother gave me permission to come with Celia and her mother," Mandie corrected him.

"I'm sorry. I know you go to school in the town where your grandmother lives and that you went to Europe with her, so I always forget that your mother is the one with the final say-so," he replied. "Anyway, I'm glad both you girls finally got here to the big city of New York, and I'm anxious to show you around."

Monet returned with a large silver tray loaded with sweet delicacies, and another maid followed with the coffee, cream and sugar, and the necessary china and silver. Monet set the tray she was carrying on a table near Mrs. Hamilton and Mr. Guyer, then she turned to help the other maid serve.

Mandie accepted a cup of coffee and noticed that Monet never said a word. The other maid inquired, "Sugar? Cream?"

As soon as the two women left the room, Mandie looked at Jonathan and started to say, "Monet doesn't—"

"Speak a word," Jonathan interrupted, finishing Mandie's sentence. "Only when it's absolutely necessary will she talk. To her it's a waste of breath." He laughed as he placed his cup of coffee on a table next to the settee.

The girls looked at him and smiled.

"You see, a mystery right here," Mandie said with a big grin.

"A mystery? No mystery about it," Jonathan said. "Monet knows how to talk. She is French, you know, and from the upper class. But she has no money, so she humbles herself to work, for a fine salary from my father, I might add. However, she feels she is above the other servants, so she refuses to converse with them. And she thinks she is being proper when she doesn't converse with her employer, either."

Mandie laughed aloud. "Oh, she should meet Liza, the maid at my mother's house," she said. "Liza would have her talking in no time flat. You've got to visit us sometime and get acquainted with everyone down our way."

"I'd like to," Jonathan said.

At that moment a tall, buxom older woman in a housekeeper's uniform appeared at the doorway to the parlor and looked directly at Mr. Guyer.

"Your guests' rooms are ready, sir," she said in a strong, no-nonsense voice with a harsh foreign accent. "Shall I show them upstairs?"

Mr. Guyer looked at Mrs. Hamilton, and she immediately said, "Yes, please, we need to get freshened up." She rose from her chair, and he also stood up.

"And I imagine you need some rest before we dine tonight," Mr. Guyer said. He looked at the housekeeper and said, "Mrs. Yodkin, please show them to their rooms and then have Monet bring them back down here at six o'clock. We'll dine at seven as usual."

"Yes, sir," the woman replied, waiting for Mrs. Hamilton and the two girls to go with her. "If there is anything you need pressed, I will have Monet do it for you," she said to Mrs. Hamilton.

"Thank you, but we'll have to see. We haven't unpacked yet," she replied.

"Monet has already unpacked your bags, madam," Mrs. Yodkin said as she turned to lead the way out of the room.

"Well, thank you," Mrs. Hamilton replied. Looking back at Mr. Guyer, she said, "Thanks for getting us out of that hotel. We appreciate your thoughtfulness."

"My pleasure, Mam'selle Jane," Mr. Guyer replied with a grin as he bowed slightly.

Mandie and Celia watched and listened in surprise. Jonathan stood by grinning.

"It has been many years since I was mam'selle, my dear monsieur," Mrs. Hamilton mischievously replied.

"Ah, but you are still that beautiful young girl in my memory," Mr. Guyer said, still grinning.

Mrs. Hamilton didn't answer but blew him a kiss with her fingers as Mrs. Yodkin, looking shocked and puzzled, continued on her way into the hallway.

"Jonathan, what is going on between my mother and your father?" Celia whispered to the boy.

"Evidently something interesting," Jonathan said with a big grin.

"Your father must know everybody," Mandie whispered as she and Celia followed Mrs. Hamilton down the hallway. Jonathan stopped and turned to go back into the parlor.

The girls got hasty glimpses into expensively furnished rooms along the way. They passed a huge library with hundreds of books covering the walls, a music room with two baby grand pianos in it, a formal drawing room, another parlor, and several closed mahogany double doors set in the wainscoting that seemed to be in every wall. They kept poking each other and exclaiming silently.

Then Mrs. Yodkin led them into a hallway that was as wide as the parlor they had been sitting in. Directly ahead of them was a carved stairway, split on either side and rising to meet again at a balcony above.

Mrs. Yodkin stopped at the bottom of the stairs and spoke to Mrs. Hamilton. "We do have an elevator over there," she said, motioning toward the left where a door with glass window panes was set in the wainscoting. "We are only going up one flight, but if madam would prefer, we can ride up."

"Oh no, thank you, Mrs. Yodkin. We need to walk, and the steps are so lovely," Mrs. Hamilton told her.

"Then we go up the stairs, madam," Mrs. Yodkin replied and started up the staircase.

When they got upstairs, Mrs. Yodkin led them from the balcony to a corridor. She showed Jane Hamilton to one room and then the girls to an adjacent room.

"Girls, get some rest and then be dressed and waiting at five-thirty," Mrs. Hamilton told them from her doorway.

"Yes, madam, five-thirty I will send Monet to direct you back to the parlor," Mrs. Yodkin said before the girls could reply. "If there is anything you need, you will find the bell rope over next to the window by the bed. Now if that is all, I will go and let you rest."

"Oh yes, Mrs. Yodkin, thank you," Mrs. Hamilton said. "And we'll be waiting for Monet."

Mrs. Yodkin slightly bowed her head, turned, and went back down the hallway.

Once inside the huge bedroom, Mandie and Celia flopped onto the two huge four-poster, canopied beds.

"What a house!" Mandie exclaimed. "I knew Jonathan's father was rich, but I didn't expect all this."

"Neither did I," Celia said. "But you know, Mandie, some people like to show off their wealth. Look at the difference in this house and your grandmother's house. She has a mansion, but nothing like this. However, I would imagine your grandmother has a lot more money than Mr. Guyer."

Mandie frowned and thought about that. "I just don't know, Celia," she said. "I know every time I turn around I find out about something else my grandmother owns, like that shipline we went to Europe on, but this house must have cost an awful lot of money to build and furnish."

Celia smiled and said, "Just think what would happen if your grandmother and Jonathan's father should get married."

Mandie sat up quickly on the bed and said, "That will never be. My grandmother doesn't even like Mr. Guyer." She paused to grin and added, "Besides, looks to me like your mother and Mr. Guyer are interested in each other."

Celia quickly shook her head and replied, "Maybe back in the old days but not now. My mother still loves my father even though she lost him last year." Her voice slightly quivered.

"I'm sorry, Celia," Mandie said. "I know it was terrible for her and for you to lose your father, just as it was for me to lose my father last year, also. But I wanted my mother to get married again, only to my uncle John, though, since he was my father's brother and I knew that my father would never be back." She paused to wipe a tear from her blue eyes.

Celia quickly jumped over to the other bed and put her arm around Mandie. Mandie straightened her slumped shoulders and asked, "Don't you think we might find some mystery in this great big house?"

Celia laughed and said, "If you're dead bent on finding one, you will."

Mandie suddenly looked around the room and asked, "Oh, where is Snowball?"

"He's probably still in the kitchen," Celia said as she, too, glanced about.

"But he should have been finished eating by now. Oh, I wonder what they've done with him," Mandie said with a frown. She slid down off the high bed and shook out her long skirts. "Maybe I'd better go see."

Celia got off the bed, too, and said, "But, Mandie, we'd never be able to find the kitchen in this house." She glanced at the windows and said, "Maybe we have one of those bell ropes like the one in my mother's room. We could ring for someone."

Mandie quickly said, "But we couldn't ring for a servant to come all the way up here just so I could ask about Snowball. No, I think I'm going to find the kitchen." She started toward the door.

"Wait, I'm going with you then," Celia told her as she rushed to follow.

The girls found their way to the staircase without any problem, but once they got to the main floor, they couldn't agree on which direction they should go.

"I'd think the kitchen would be to one side or the other from here," Celia said as they stood in the hallway at the foot of the stairs.

"Oh no, Celia, it would be at the back of the house, somewhere beyond this staircase," Mandie replied, then she walked over to look around one set of stairs.

"But, Mandie, this staircase is at the back of the house when you think about how long the hallway is leading up to it," Celia told her.

"Come on. Let's look in some of these rooms," Mandie said. She stepped over to a closed door in the narrow piece of corridor that went past the staircase.

"Mandie, what if we open the door to someone's private room?" Celia asked in a whisper.

"Then we can just say, 'excuse me,' and ask whoever it is where the kitchen is," Mandie replied in a loud whisper. She cautiously pushed open the door and peeped inside. Long mahogany tables were piled high with fabric, and two sewing machines stood by the double windows across the room. She pulled the door shut. "Nobody there. Just a sewing room."

The girls opened and closed several more doors but found only small parlors, a storage room for linens, and a small sitting room with a carved mahogany desk in it. They did not hear or see anyone.

"I think we'd better go back in the other direction," Celia told her.

"Just one more. I see one more door," Mandie said, hurrying to open a door at the end of a center hallway. "Oh, look what I found!" she exclaimed as she stepped through the doorway.

Celia followed. They were in a huge room full of growing plants and several small flowing water fountains with various statues standing guard. The ceiling and three of the walls were made of glass. A fresh, cool scent filled the air.

Mandie walked on the stone floor, stopping to finger the long green stems growing here and there and to smell fresh peppermint plants and tiny buds sprouting out in the midst of the jungle-like room.

"This is a beautiful place!" Celia exclaimed.

"I wonder if Snowball could be in here," Mandie said as she tried to see between the plants. "Snow ball! Kitty, kitty! Come here, Snowball."

"Mandie, I don't think Snowball would be in here. He's supposed to be in the kitchen," Celia reminded her.

"Yes, supposed to be," Mandie said. "There's no telling what that French maid did with him. Remember, she seemed afraid of him. He could have run away from her."

Footsteps sounded across the room on the other side of the tall plants. Both girls stopped and waited to see who was there. And in a moment they were surprised to see Jonathan coming toward them.

"I knew you two wouldn't stay in your room," Jonathan said with a big grin.

"Oh, Jonathan, we only came down here to look for Snowball," Mandie explained. "I forgot to get him back from your maid after she fed him."

"In that case, he's probably still in the kitchen. Come on. We'll go look," Jonathan told her.

"We couldn't find the kitchen," Celia said as they left the room through a different door from the first one they had come through.

"It's right here," Jonathan said, looking back at the girls as he opened a heavy wooden door directly across the small hallway they had entered.

"What a kitchen!" Mandie exclaimed as the three of them stepped inside a huge room furnished with three of the very latest in cookstoves, several work tables upon which were utensils and equipment for cooking, an enormous pantry through an open door in the far corner, various bins and stools, and shelves and shelves of chinaware.

"It is rather big, isn't it? But then when my father entertains for a dinner of maybe a hundred people, this room doesn't seem large enough to take care of the necessary food that is cooked," Jonathan explained.

"A hundred people?" Mandie said in surprise. "Where do that many people eat?"

"Oh, we have three dining rooms, each with a movable wall that can be opened into one large room," he replied.

"I'm just plumb overcome with this huge house," Celia told him.

Mandie suddenly realized the odor of cooking food filled the room. She sniffed and looked around. "Where is the food being cooked?" she asked.

"Oh, it's in all the ovens over there, and it will be ready for us to eat tonight," Jonathan told her, gesturing toward the stoves.

At that moment, a short, hefty woman with eyeglasses perched on her long nose came into the room through a door on the far side. When she saw them, the woman stopped and put her hands on her hips, which were covered with a large white apron. "Now, now, Master Jonathan, we came to an understanding, just yesterday it was, that you would not come to raid my kitchen any more," she said as she shook a long finger at him.

Jonathan laughed, and the girls laughed with him. "But I'm not bothering your cooking, Mrs. Cook. I'm only looking for that white cat you were supposed to feed," he said.

"White cat? Oh yes, I fed that white cat, and he ate like he'd not had a bite today. Shame, shame for starving the poor fellow," Mrs. Cook said, shaking her head.

Mandie laughed again and said, "But Snowbal eats like that all the time, no matter how much I feed him. He never gets full. Where is he, Mrs. Cook?"

"Why, I suppose he's still out in the garden. That French maid didn't want anything to do with him and decided he needed to go outside," Mrs. Cook explained.

"Oh no!" Mandie said with a loud gasp.

"Come on. We'll go find him. The garden is closed in with a gate, so he's probably still out there," Jonathan said, quickly leading the way through the kitchen, down a short hall, and then opening the back door.

"Jonathan, Snowball is a cat, and cats climb. You can't fence them in," Mandie said with a moan as she and Celia followed. "Oh, I hope I can find him."

As they stepped into the backyard, the three of them began searching among the shrubbery and plants that were interspersed with more statues and fountains like the ones in the glass room. Benches stood among the foliage. The garden was enclosed with a high stone wall, but Mandie found the gate standing wide open, and outside was a street with busy traffic.

"Snowball, Snowball, where are you? Kitty, kitty!" she called as she stepped outside the gate to look for her cat. There was no sign of him, so she came back inside the garden and pulled the gate closed. And when she did, she heard a faint growl. She glanced behind a nearby bush and couldn't believe what she had found. "Snowball!"

"Did you find him?" Celia asked as she and Jonathan came to see what Mandie was doing.

"Look!" Mandie excitedly told her friends.

Snowball was standing there hissing at a white dog, much larger than he was, sitting behind the gate when Mandie had swung it shut. The dog looked terrified of the cat.

"I wonder whose dog that is," Jonathan said, stooping to look at the animal, whose eyes were fastened on the white cat. Snowball paid no attention to his mistress.

"I never saw a dog afraid of a cat before," Celia remarked.

"He has a collar on," Jonathan said, moving closer to the dog. Then, looking up, he said, "Mandie, how about shooing your cat away so I can look at the poor fellow's collar."

Mandie laughed and, reaching down, quickly picked up Snowball, who didn't like the idea at all and tried to escape from her arms. "No more dog chasing, Snowball," she told him as he wriggled.

Jonathan quickly examined the collar on the dog that was still too afraid to move. "Poor fellow, I won't let that mean cat terrify you any more," he said, slowly touching the collar. Then the dog suddenly began licking Jonathan's hand.

Mandie and Celia watched as Jonathan carefully turned the collar around. It was almost completely covered with blue, red, and green glass stones.

"No identification," Jonathan said in a disappointed voice as he stroked the dog's head.

"What are you going to do with him, Jonathan?" Celia asked.

"Do? Why, I just don't know," Jonathan replied. "I've never seen him before. I have no idea."

"Well, you can't just turn him out into the street. He's so meek there's no telling what would happen to him," Mandie said.

"Evidently that's where he came from," Jonathan replied.

"Your father said he heard it was going to snow,"

Celia reminded him. "He might freeze to death out here in the snow."

"You could let him stay on the back porch. It's closed in enough so he wouldn't be out in the cold," Mandie suggested.

"He looks so clean. Someone must have given him a bath not long ago," Jonathan said as he continued rubbing the dog's fur. "I suppose he could stay on the back porch until something can be done about him."

Jonathan stood up, and as he did, the dog also rose. Walking toward the porch, the dog followed right on Jonathan's heels.

Mandie smiled and said, "I believe he likes you, Jonathan."

"Well, I don't want him to like me too much because I know he must belong to someone else and wouldn't be able to keep him," Jonathan said, continuing toward the porch.

The girls followed. Mandie had to hold tightly to Snowball, who was determined to get down.

"Mandie, we should go back to our room now," Celia reminded her.

As they all stepped onto the back porch, Mandie agreed. "Yes, Jonathan, we're supposed to be in our room resting. We only came down to find Snowball," she said. "We'll be back down at six like your father asked."

"All right," Jonathan said, carefully closing the outside door to the porch and latching it. "I'll get doggie something to eat and see you then." The dog stayed close by.

As the girls entered the house with Jonathan, he headed for the kitchen, and then Mandie remembered they didn't know the way back to the staircase to go to their room. "Jonathan, wait," she said. "How do we get back upstairs?"

"Simple," he said as he pushed open a door in the back hallway.

Mandie could see the staircase from there and laughed as she and Celia headed for it. "All the time we were wandering around looking for the kitchen we must have been right at it," she said.

"I know. Remember that's what I kept telling you all the time?" Celia reminded her as they hurried up the stairs.

"I remember, but we had a nice tour of the house anyway, didn't we?" Mandie said, holding tightly to Snowball.

"Yes, and I can imagine what would have happened if you and I had been caught in the kitchen without Jonathan. I don't think Mrs. Cook would have been very pleased with us," Celia said.

Moving quickly down the hallway to their room, Mandie stopped and said, "And we do have a mystery. Where did the dog come from? Who does he belong to?"

"Oh, come on, Mandie," Celia told her as she continued on to their room and opened the door.

Mandie hurried to catch up. "Yes, we can figure that all out later."

Chapter 3 / The Strange Girl

Mandie set Snowball down on the carpet in the room she was sharing with Celia and then flopped on one of the beds. Celia was already on the other bed.

"Do you think Jonathan will keep the white dog?" Celia asked.

"If he can't find the owner, his father may not allow him to keep it," Mandie said. "He has never owned a pet, you know. So I just don't know what will happen to the poor dog if we can't solve the mystery."

"He is a beautiful dog. I wouldn't mind having him, but I know my mother would say we have enough animals back home," Celia told her. "Anyhow, I think—"

"Snowball!" Mandie suddenly interrupted Celia as she jumped up from the bed. Snowball was running around in circles and making loud growling noises. "What is wrong with you?" She bent down to get a look at him. He meowed and continued rushing around the room.

"What is wrong?" Celia asked, excitedly joining Mandie.

"A sandbox. He wants a sandbox, that's it. Oh, where is the sandbox?" Mandie exclaimed, growing excited herself as she raced about the room looking for one.

"Mandie, there isn't one in here," Celia told her.

"Isn't one? Oh, how could we forget to ask for one?" Mandie replied as she tried to figure out what to do next.

"Take him back outside," Celia told her.

"I'd never find the way in time," Mandie said as she bent to pick up the cat. "I'll put him in the bathtub. You ring the bell for the servants fast."

Mandie quickly carried Snowball into the bathroom and set him down in the tub as Celia raced for the bell cord. The cat was puzzled by his mistress's actions and meowed as he raced around inside the bathtub. He tried to jump out, but Mandie pushed him back down.

Remembering that Celia's mother was in her room on the other side of the bathroom and was probably taking a nap, Mandie whispered to Celia through their open door, "Did you ring?"

Celia came to the doorway and whispered back, "Yes, I pulled and pulled. I'm sure it rang downstairs or wherever it's connected."

"Well, I wish somebody would hurry," Mandie said, bending over the tub. "Snowball, you just stay down there."

At last a knock sounded on the door to the hallway. Celia rushed to open it. There stood the maid who had helped Monet serve coffee in the parlor.

"Oh, thank goodness you are here," Celia said, stepping back to allow the woman to come into the room. "In the bathroom."

The woman looked at her in puzzlement and walked to the bathroom door.

"I'm so glad to see you," Mandie said. "You see, we should have had a sandbox put in our room for my cat to use, but we forgot all about it. Now he has need for one, and I can't find the way out of the house to let him in the backyard."

"Oh, zat ees all," the woman said and reached for a towel. "Just geeve him to Zelda. I take him out." She picked up the cat, wrapped the big towel around him, and started back through the room to the hall door.

"Wait!" Mandie called to her as she ran to a table and picked up the cat's red leash. "I have to put this on him or he might run away if he goes outside."

The woman stopped and looked at the leash in Mandie's hand. "But he ees not a dog," she said.

"But he still likes to run away," Mandie said, fastening the leash to his red collar. "I'll go with you."

As Mandie followed Zelda out the door, Celia called, "Don't be too long. We have to get dressed pretty soon."

"As soon as I can find out where to get a sandbox, I'll be back," Mandie replied.

Zelda led the way through the house and out to the backyard, where she set Snowball down. He immediately began scratching around in the dirt. Mandie held on to the end of his leash.

"Could somebody get us a box with sand in it to take up to our room for Snowball to use next time?" Mandie asked the woman, who stood watching the cat.

"Box weeth sand?" Zelda asked. "Sand ees out here."

"Yes, a box with sand in it for his bathroom," Mandie tried to explain. "Come to think of it, I wonder if Jonathan realizes that dog might mess up the back porch?" She tried to see through the garden to the back porch. Zelda had brought them outside through another door that opened into a patio.

Zelda didn't reply but stood there still watching the cat.

"Do you know where Jonathan is? Could you tell him I'm out here in the backyard?" Mandie asked.

Zelda didn't seem to understand what Mandie wanted and kept looking at her.

Mandie tried again. "Jonathan? Get him," she said slowly.

"Get zee leetle man," Zelda finally replied. She shook her head and turned back to the house. "Get zee leetle man." She went inside.

In a few minutes Jonathan came rushing out the door. "What's wrong?" he asked, hurrying over to her.

"We don't have a sandbox for Snowball in our room, and we almost didn't get down here in time," Mandie told him.

"Oh, I'm so sorry. I should have thought of that," Jonathan said. Then with a big grin he added, "I will ask Monet to put one together and deliver it to your room right away."

"Monet? But, Jonathan—" Mandie began.

"Yes, Monet," he repeated. "I like to bring her down to earth now and then and make her realize she is being paid to work." He grinned.

"That is downright mean of you, Jonathan,"

Mandie replied as she moved around holding the end of the leash. "If you'll get me some kind of container, I will make a sandbox myself."

"Oh no, as my father would say, Monet will," Jonathan promised as he went back toward the door into the house. "You will have a sandbox shortly."

Mandie stopped him as she called, "Wait! I don't know the way back to our room. I think Snowball is all right now."

"Come on then," Jonathan replied.

Mandie picked up Snowball and she followed Jonathan into the house, through two different hallways, and finally to the staircase.

"Thanks, I know the way from here," Mandie told him.

"One sandbox coming up," Jonathan promised as he walked down the hallway.

When she got back to their room, Mandie explained to Celia how Jonathan was going to get a sandbox.

"I didn't realize Jonathan could act like that," Mandie said in a disappointed voice as she sat on a chair nearby.

"But you know, Mandie, he is absolutely right. If Monet is being paid to work, then she should work for the money," Celia said.

"But I could have made a sandbox if he would have given me something to put the sand in," Mandie said. "Besides, he could have, too. I think he has just got plain lazy since he came home to New York. He wasn't like that when we met him on the ship."

"I think we'd better start getting dressed," Celia reminded her.

"I reckon so," Mandie said. She rose and went

to find a dress in the tall wardrobe.

While the girls were dressing, Monet brought up the sandbox, which she silently placed in a corner of the bedroom. Without a word she turned and left the room.

"Thank you," Mandie told Monet as she went out the door, but the prim maid didn't even let on that she heard her.

When Monet had closed the door behind her, Mandie sighed and said, "Oh well, I really do thank her."

The girls and Mrs. Hamilton were dressed and waiting when the housekeeper herself came back and escorted them down to the parlor. Jonathan and his father were waiting there for them, and Mandie couldn't believe her eyes. The white dog was lying on the hearth by the fire and looked as though he had had a bath.

"Jonathan?" Mandie asked as she and Celia walked straight over to the settee where Jonathan had risen at their entrance.

"Do you like my dog?" Jonathan asked, mischievously grinning as the three of them sat on the settee. Mrs. Hamilton joined Mr. Guyer by the fireplace.

"Are you going to keep him?" Mandie asked.

"Did your father say you could?" Celia wanted to know.

"Yes, my father said I could keep him—until someone comes along to claim him, which I certainly hope won't happen," Jonathan explained to the girls. "I gave him a hot bath. He was cold out there on the back porch. Now he can stay in the house and will only go into the backyard when he has to."

"I'm so glad for you," Celia said.

"It's a good thing I left Snowball in our room. Remember, he's afraid of my cat," Mandie said with a grin.

"Oh, but you could have brought him down here. There's plenty of room for them both," Jonathan replied.

"No, seriously, Jonathan, it would not have been nice for me to bring my cat down here to the parlor. After all, we are only guests in your father's house, and there are so many things Snowball could get into or break," Mandie said. "We left him asleep on the hearth by the fire in our room. And Monet did bring the sandbox."

"And speaking of Monet, here she is," Jonathan said under his breath as the maid wheeled a cart holding coffee, tea, and sweet cakes into the room and parked it near Mr. Guyer.

"Just leave it here, Monet," Mr. Guyer said. "We'll help ourselves."

Monet silently left the room. Mr. Guyer spoke to Mrs. Hamilton as he stood up by the cart, "Please tell me what you would like."

Mrs. Hamilton also rose, assisted him with the coffee, and told the young people to come over and get what they wanted.

"Monet seems peeved about something. Maybe it's that dog I allowed Jonathan to bring into the house, but I didn't think we needed her sullen attitude to spoil our evening," Mr. Guyer told Mrs. Hamilton as they sat back down.

The three young people overheard the remarks, and Mandie whispered under her breath, "Your father doesn't know about the sandbox."

"No, and don't tell him," Jonathan whispered back.

Mr. Guyer glanced at them and asked, "And what are you whispering about, Jonathan?"

"These are really delicious-looking sweet cakes," Mandie said, quickly putting one on a small plate. "Did your cook make them, Mr. Guyer?"

"Why, yes, as a matter of fact, Mrs. Cook did bake them," Mr. Guyer replied. Then he smiled and added, "I'm sure you will enjoy them, but that couldn't be what Jonathan was whispering about."

"Father, please!" Jonathan exclaimed as he also took one of the sweet cakes.

"Oh, it was private then," Mr. Guyer replied with a grin so much like Jonathan's. He turned back to Mrs. Hamilton and said, "It was nice to be young and have secrets from our parents, wasn't it?"

"Yes, and I did have lots of secrets," Mrs. Hamilton replied as she drank her coffee.

Celia heard that and said under her breath, "Secrets? And she has never wanted me to have a single secret."

"Pay no attention to those two old people over there. We have other more interesting things to talk about," Jonathan said with another grin as they all sat down again with their refreshments.

"Like seeing New York," Mandie said, smiling.

"Yes, we must make plans for tomorrow," Jonathan said.

"I think my mother wants to go shopping tomorrow," Celia said.

"Then we'll go shopping and stop here and there to sight-see," Jonathan told her. "I'll show you Broadway and Saint Patrick's Cathedral. The church is huge and really beautiful. And maybe we'll get to ride in my father's motorcar."

"Your father's motorcar?" Mandie said. "He owns a motorcar?"

"Right, and as soon as I am old enough, I will be able to drive it," Jonathan said. "In the meantime, if my father is not around to drive it, then we will have to ask Jens to take us."

"I'd much rather ride in one of those horsecars, I believe you call them, that go up and down Fifth Avenue," Mandie said.

"Well, I have to be different and say I'd rather just walk," Celia said.

"New York is too big and crowded to walk much. Besides, what will you do with all the packages of things you and your mother will buy? You can't just carry them around with you," Jonathan said.

"Now, Jonathan, I happen to know the best stores will deliver whatever you buy right up to the front door. You can't mislead me into getting into that motorcar," Celia said with a teasing smile.

"You know too much, Celia," Jonathan teased back.

"Anyhow, we will have to consult with Celia's mother before we can make any plans for tomorrow," Mandie said.

The white dog rose from the hearth and came over to put his head on Jonathan's knee. "Now, isn't that nice?" Jonathan said, patting the dog's fur. "He already knows who his master is."

Mandie smiled and said, "I would suggest you let him check out the backyard now and then until he gets used to staying in the house."

Jonathan understood what she meant. "You mean—like Snowball?" he asked.

Mandie nodded, and he quickly rose. She put

down her coffee cup on a table and said, "Wait. I'll go with you."

Mrs. Hamilton saw them rise and start toward the door with the dog. "Where are you going, Amanda?" she asked.

"Just out in the yard with Jonathan and the dog," Mandie replied.

"Not without a coat," Mrs. Hamilton said firmly. "It's cold out there."

Mandie remembered the maid had hung their coats on the hall tree, and she quickly looked to see if they were still there. "Our wraps are here," she told Mrs. Hamilton as she took her coat off the hook and put it on. Jonathan took a coat that evidently belonged to him from another hook.

"Well, I suppose I might as well go, too," Celia said, coming to join them and get her coat.

Mrs. Hamilton watched them and said, "Hats, too, girls."

After the three of them were dressed for the cold, Jonathan spoke to the dog and he followed them through the house and out the back door into the garden.

Mandie took a quick breath upon stepping outside. "Your mother was right, Celia. It is cold out here," she said.

"Right," Celia agreed, turning up the collar of her coat.

Several outside lights gave a faint illumination to the garden, and as soon as the door closed behind them, the dog raced to the gate in the fence. The young people followed.

"Come on back, feller. You can't go out into the street. The gate's closed anyhow," Jonathan called to the dog.

As they reached the gate, a voice called to them from the other side, "Let my dog out of there right now!"

The three young people stopped in surprise. Mandie was the first one to spot the girl sitting on top of the wall by the gate in the dark.

"Who are you?" Mandie asked.

"Yes, who are you, and what are you doing on my property?" Jonathan asked as they came up to the wall.

"I want my dog," the girl said angrily. "Let him out."

Mandie glanced at the white dog. He was exploring a bush nearby and completely ignoring the girl. "If this is your dog, how come he doesn't seem to know you?" she asked, squinting to see the girl better.

The girl jumped down from the wall and landed near where the young people were standing. "Give me my dog," she insisted, looking around for the animal.

As the girl moved into a better light, Mandie could see that her clothes were raggedy and that she did not have on enough warm clothes in the cold weather. The girl did not look older than ten years.

"You will have to prove you own this dog," Jonathan told her as he watched her closely.

"Come on, Fido," the girl said to the dog as she took hold of his collar and tried to pull him toward the gate. The dog jerked back and went running off to another part of the garden. The girl went after him. "Fido, come back here," she called.

The young people followed her, and Jonathan spoke sternly, "Now, you look here, miss, if you don't leave this property I will call my father, and I am sure he will call the authorities."

The girl stopped instantly and turned to him. "He wouldn't do that now, would he? That's my dog you got here," she insisted.

"Yes, he would do that," Jonathan said. "Now, I will let you out the gate. If you come back tomorrow with some proof that this dog belongs to you, I will let you have him, but you are not going to take him tonight."

The girl pushed her dark, stringy hair back under her hat, shook an ungloved fist at Jonathan, and said, "I will be back tomorrow and get my dog." She raced over to the gate, tried to open it, and found it locked.

"I'll get the key," Jonathan said and hurried toward the back porch.

Mandie watched and noticed that he did not go into the house but retrieved the key from somewhere around the back porch. He came back and unlocked the gate.

"Now, you come to the door proper when you do come back. No more sneaking over the wall," Jonathan told her, but she didn't seem to listen to a word he was saying. As soon as he swung the gate open, she raced through and disappeared into the dark street.

Jonathan locked the gate, and the three of them went back inside the house with the white dog.

"Do you think that dog really belongs to that girl?" Mandie asked. She noticed Jonathan had put the key in his pocket.

"No, I don't believe it. The dog ignored her," Jonathan replied as they went along a hallway. "Come on, feller," he urged the dog.

"I don't, either, but how did she know you had the dog?" Mandie asked.

"Maybe she saw it come into our garden earlier today," Jonathan said.

"She looked too poor to afford to keep a dog," Celia remarked.

When they returned to the parlor, Jonathan told his father about the girl. "I just don't think the dog could belong to her," Jonathan concluded.

"She may know where the dog came from and decided to claim it for herself," Mr. Guyer said. "Don't worry about it. She would have to have proof of ownership before I'd let her have it."

"Thanks, Father," Jonathan replied.

No more was said about the dog that evening, and when it was time to retire, Mr. Guyer told Jonathan, "I would suggest you let the dog sleep in your room tonight so you will know where he is. We can't have him roaming all over the house."

"Of course, Father," Jonathan agreed with a big grin. "He can sleep on the rug right beside my bed, and I will see that my door is closed."

When good-nights were said and the girls were alone in their room, Mandie thought about the girl as she undressed for bed.

"I wish we could help that girl. She looked like she could use some better clothes," she said to Celia, who was already combing out her hair for the night.

"I know," Celia agreed. "Maybe there's some way we can help her."

Mandie drifted off to sleep that night wondering where the dog really came from and who the girl was. These things needed to be cleared up.

Chapter 4 / What a Day!

Mandie was always an early riser, and she woke the next morning just as a maid came into the room she was sharing with Celia and quietly built up the fire in the fireplace, even though the great mansion had furnace heat going.

The maid, a young girl whom Mandie had never seen, looked up from where she was stooping by the fireplace as Mandie sat up in bed and said, "Good morning."

"Guten morgan," the girl quickly replied with a big smile as she shuffled the wood.

Mandie jumped out of bed and came to join her. "German!" she said. "You are German. I know because I went to Germany with my grandmother this past summer, and that is the way the German people say good morning." Mandie grinned as she wrapped the loose nightgown around herself and sat on the carpet.

"Ja!" the girl replied shyly.

"And that means yes," Mandie said. "But please don't say too much more in German because I don't know very much. You do speak English, don't you?"

"Ja, I speak American language," the girl replied.

Celia had silently crawled out of her bed and joined them. She said, "Mr. Guyer has so many people working here, and they're all different nationalities." She flopped down by Mandie.

"German, French, Russian is all, and American," the girl explained.

"So Zelda must be Russian. I couldn't figure her out," Mandie said. "My name is Mandie Shaw. What is yours?" She wondered how old the girl was and decided she must not be much older than her own thirteen years.

"I am called Leila," the girl said as she rose and pushed back her long reddish-blond hair and adjusted the tiny maid's cap on her head. She was young but she was tall and a little on the plump side. "I will go now," she added, turning toward the door.

Mandie and Celia stood up by the fire and at that moment Snowball, who had been asleep in the middle of Mandie's bed, jumped down and came running to join the girls by the fireplace.

"Ah! He is the cat for the sandbox," Leila exclaimed as she watched him. "Nice, pretty."

"Thank you," Mandie said. "His name is Snowball, and he belongs to me. I take him with me everywhere I go."

"Does Snowball like the white dog Master Jonathan has in his room?" Leila asked.

Mandie laughed as she replied, "That white dog is afraid of Snowball."

"Is Jonathan already up?" Celia asked. "Has he gone out yet?"

"Up and down the stairs with the white dog," Leila said as she opened the door. "Now I fix fire in next room." She went out into the hallway and closed the door behind her.

"Let's get dressed and see if we can find Jonathan," Mandie said, rushing to open the huge wardrobe.

"And find something to eat," Celia added as she followed.

Just as the girls were buttoning their dresses and smoothing out their long skirts, there was a soft knock on the door.

"Now, who can that be?" Mandie said, going to open the door.

The maid, Zelda, stood there in the hallway holding a silver tray. She came into the room and said, "Drink. Eat in half hour. I come back then." She set the tray on a table nearby, and Mandie could see then that two crystal glasses full of orange juice stood beside a bud vase holding a bright red rose.

"Thank you," Mandie told the maid as she left the room.

"This is nice," Celia said, picking up one of the glasses and drinking from it.

"Yes, I agree," Mandie said, taking the other one and sitting on a chair nearby. "I just wonder if we could find Jonathan."

"Mandie, we might get lost, and Zelda said she would be back for us in thirty minutes," Celia reminded her. "Besides, my mother is in the next room, remember, and we can't go running off without letting her know."

"I'll be glad to find out what plans your mother

has for us today," Mandie said.

"We still have to finish getting ready," Celia reminded her.

When Mandie and Celia were finally ready, the door opened to the bathroom between the two rooms, and Celia's mother came into their room.

The girls both eagerly greeted her with "Good morning" and "What are we doing today?"

Mrs. Hamilton smiled at them and said, "Well, for pity's sake, y'all make me feel so important I'm speechless." She sat down on a chair near the girls.

"Oh, Mother, please tell us. Are we going shopping or sightseeing today?" Celia asked eagerly.

"I thought we'd do some of both," Jane replied.

"Oh, thank you, Mrs. Hamilton. That's exactly what Jonathan suggested, and that's what we want to do," Mandie told her.

"I'm not real interested in shopping, but I'll go along just to do the sightseeing," Celia teased. "Besides, I don't have any money."

"Celia, of course you have money. I brought enough for you to buy some new clothes and other things if you'd like," Mrs. Hamilton told her in surprise. Then turning to Mandie, she asked, "Did your mother give you spending money?"

"Oh yes, ma'am," Mandie told her. "I have a whole purse full of money, but I have no idea what I'll do with it."

"Everything in New York is expensive, so you won't have any trouble getting rid of it," Mrs. Hamilton said with a smile.

There was a knock on the door, and Celia opened it. Zelda was standing there in the hallway.

"You eat now," the maid said, looking into the room and seeing Mrs. Hamilton. "We go."

"Oh yes, thank you," Mrs. Hamilton said.

Mandie quickly put Snowball in the bathroom and closed the door. Then they followed the woman downstairs to the dining room. Jonathan was waiting for them by the huge sliding doors made of mahogany to match the wainscoting.

"Good morning," he greeted Mrs. Hamilton. "My father left his regrets, but he received a telephone call during the night and had to go down to Washington early this morning. He hopes to return by tomorrow night and should be home for Thanksgiving dinner, which is the day after tomorrow. I'm sorry."

"I'm sorry we'll miss his company, but I understand," Mrs. Hamilton said as Jonathan stepped aside and motioned for her to enter the dining room.

The three of them and Jonathan were seated at a long table covered with white linen and set with the finest china and silverware. A silver candelabra stood at each end. They made their plans for the day while the housekeeper, Mrs. Yodkin, stood by supervising the serving of the meal.

"My father told me to ask Jens to drive us in the motorcar wherever you wish to go," Jonathan said. "Jens is the butler, you know, and he can drive the motorcar, but Hodson drives the carriage."

"Thank you, Jonathan, but I think the carriage would be more practical for us to use," Mrs. Hamilton told him.

"And more comfortable," Jonathan agreed with a big grin.

Mandie and Celia looked at each other and breathed sighs of relief. They listened as Mrs. Hamilton and Jonathan mapped out their day, and everyone began filling their plates with food.

"Will I be able to take Snowball with me?" Mandie asked.

"Why don't you leave him here, Amanda? Some of the stores probably won't allow pets inside," Mrs. Hamilton told her as she took a roll from the basket the maid was holding.

"Yes, and New York is awfully big for him to get lost in. We'd never find him," Jonathan added as he took a sip of coffee.

"Then I'll have to feed him and shut him up in our room. I hope no one lets him out," Mandie said. "Where is the white dog, Jonathan?"

"He's in the kitchen, where he's going to stay until we return. Mrs. Cook has made friends with him," Jonathan explained.

"What if that girl comes back to claim him while we're gone?" Mandie asked as she accepted potatoes from a tray being passed. Then she suddenly glanced down at what she had put on her plate. *These people eat potatoes for breakfast!* she thought. *How odd!* She looked around and saw that Celia and Mrs. Hamilton had both put potatoes on their plates.

"She won't be able to get him because Mrs. Cook has strict orders not to let him outside except when absolutely necessary, and then with strict supervision," Jonathan replied. "She'll just have to come back when I'm home. I'm sorry for the inconvenience to her, but I can't stay home all day waiting for her to show up when she may never even come back."

"Are you hoping that she doesn't?" Celia asked.

Jonathan grinned and said, "Sure, I'm hoping she won't be able to claim him, or that anyone else ever will. I'm positive he must belong to someone, but I don't believe that girl owns him."

"We never did ask her where she lives or her name," Mandie said.

"No, and that was a big mistake. I could have had someone check her out," Jonathan said.

"The girl may never come back," Mrs. Hamilton told him. "Surely she has some parents or somebody somewhere to see that she doesn't go running around on the streets alone at night in New York."

"Anyhow, right now we've got things to do, like sightseeing," Celia reminded them as she hurriedly ate her breakfast.

"Yes, the dog is safe, so let's get finished and get going," Mandie agreed. She wasn't very hungry and had taken small portions of the food when it was passed.

They were soon on their way in the carriage. Jonathan instructed Hodson to drive slowly and be prepared to stop and let them out to walk around now and then.

Their first stop was St. Patrick's Cathedral. The girls were greatly impressed with the magnificent Gothic Revival style church as Jonathan acted as tour guide.

"This church took twenty-six years to build," he told them as they stood on the sidewalk in front of it on Fifth Avenue. "It is a whole block long, from Fiftieth Street to Fifty-first Street." He motioned up and down the street.

"How old is it?" Mandie asked as she leaned backward trying to see to the top of the spire in front of her.

"It was opened for service in 1879, and it is now 1901. But remember, it took all those years to build, so I suppose you'd calculate the age by what was constructed in what year," he explained, becoming confused in his thought.

"In other words, pieces of it are actually older than others," Celia said with a mischievous grin.

"Why don't we look inside?" Mrs. Hamilton told the young people as she walked up the steps to the huge doors.

Jonathan rushed ahead to open the door, then he followed the girls and Mrs. Hamilton inside, where they paused at the back to look around.

Mandie could feel the peaceful atmosphere as she gazed about at the beautiful carved woodwork and stained glass windows. She stepped forward to look more closely at a pew when a dark form suddenly darted between the seats. She quickly moved in that direction to investigate.

"Amanda, where are you going?" Mrs. Hamilton asked in a whisper.

Jonathan had also noticed the movement, and he hurried after Mandie, who had not heard Mrs. Hamilton's question.

"That's the girl who came to your house!" Mandie whispered to Jonathan as she finally got a good look at the moving form.

Jonathan followed her gaze, but at that moment Mrs. Hamilton stepped forward and sternly caught Mandie by the hand. Without a word she swiftly pushed Mandie and Celia back to the outside door and Jonathan followed.

"There are people praying in there," Mrs. Hamilton scolded the young people. "We can't go running around and disturbing them."

"But I saw that girl in there who claimed the white dog," Mandie replied. Mrs. Hamilton frowned at her. "I'm sorry," Mandie continued.

"I think we'd better go now," Mrs. Hamilton said.

They returned to the carriage to continue their sightseeing, and Mandie could tell that Mrs. Hamilton was upset by her behavior. She didn't know what else to say, so she tried to remain silent, but her friends wanted to talk.

"Do you really think that was the girl in our backyard last night?" Jonathan asked as Hodson drove on.

"I'm positive it was, but she saw us and tried to run away and hide," Mandie said.

"I got a glimpse of her, too," Celia said. "It was the same girl."

"Well, it was a little dark in there after being outside in the sunshine, so I couldn't tell who it was," Jonathan explained.

"I wonder what she was doing in there," Celia commented.

"Anyone can go into a church," Jonathan said. "It was probably just a coincidence that we met up with her."

"Or she could live in the neighborhood near the church and saw us go inside and decided to follow," Mandie suggested.

The driver pulled the carriage to a stop in front of a large building on West Fifty-seventh Street. They all left the vehicle and looked around.

Jonathan quickly began explaining, "This is Carnegie Hall. It is rather new. It only opened about ten years ago."

"Well, what is it?" Mandie asked, glimpsing at the colorful posters around the doorway. She tried the doors but discovered they were locked.

"It's a music hall, I suppose you'd call it," he said. "Some very well-known musicians and actors perform here from time to time. And you can only go inside when there is something going on, and then you have to have a ticket to get in."

"We won't have time to attend a concert here," Mrs. Hamilton told them. "Maybe next time we come to New York. I think we'd better go on downtown, Jonathan, if we're going to do any shopping today."

"Oh yes, ma'am," Jonathan replied as they returned to the carriage. "I'll tell Hodson where to go."

"And, Jonathan, we will need to find a place to eat somewhere in the shopping district," Jane replied. She and the girls entered the carriage. Jonathan gave instructions to the driver and then joined them.

"I asked Hodson to drive through Longacre Square on the way," Jonathan told Mrs. Hamilton.

"Thank you, Jonathan. I'm sure it will be an interesting sight for the girls to see," she replied.

"What is Longacre Square?" Mandie asked.

"It's the busiest section of New York. It's where everything and almost everybody come together. It's where Forty-second Street and Seventh Avenue and Broadway cross each other," Jonathan explained.

As the carriage continued down Broadway to what Jonathan called Longacre Square, both girls eagerly watched the crowds hurrying here and there. Stores and theaters were all tightly built together side-by-side. Vehicles and motorcars mingling with carriages rushed in what appeared to be every direction.

"Oh, you're right, Jonathan. Everything and everybody in New York must be out there," Mandie said without glancing away from the scene outside the carriage.

"I don't think I'd like to walk out there," Celia remarked.

"No, it's not a place to take a leisurely stroll," Mrs. Hamilton said.

And as they went from one huge store to another to do their shopping, the girls were interested in the sizes of the buildings. Once they were inside, they were pushed and shoved by the rush of shoppers until they learned how to weave in and out of the crowds behind Mrs. Hamilton. Then they saw the beautiful merchandise, things Mandie had never seen in any store. There were ready-made dresses in every shape, color, and size.

"How can they sell dresses all made up like that? Suppose no one ever comes along that they will fit?" Mandie said as she stopped to look.

Mrs. Hamilton smiled at her and said, "Oh, but they have so many different sizes, and if you look around you'll see the customers are all different sizes."

"But I still don't think these dresses would fit as well as the ones Aunt Lou makes for me," Mandie said, walking the length of the clothes rack, not daring to touch the dresses.

"You are right about that," Mrs. Hamilton told her. "Nothing ready-made ever fits as well as your own seamstress's work."

Mandie wasn't interested in buying any of the expensive merchandise she saw until they entered a hat shop. She and Celia went wild over the huge assortment of hats.

"Oh, I must buy a hat," Mandie said, walking around the shop. "You know, Celia, it's impossible to find a store like this back home.''

"I want one, too,'' Celia replied as she surveyed the stock.

Jonathan smiled at them as he watched and listened. "I know,'' he teased. "You girls just want to look older.''

Mandie turned to him and said, "Well, we are getting older, you know, old enough to wear hats.'' She looked at a simple but expensive hat trimmed with red ribbons.

"I agree with you, Amanda,'' Mrs. Hamilton said, coming to stand beside the girls. "You and Celia do need to buy something in keeping with your age. As much as I hate to admit it, you two are growing into young ladies. Let me help y'all find something.''

They shopped the rest of the day, taking time only to eat in a nearby restaurant. Everything they bought was to be delivered the next day to Jonathan's house. Early winter dusk was beginning to cover New York as Hodson drove them back to Jonathan's house. Everyone was tired and silent.

As soon as they entered the house, Jonathan told the girls, "I have to go see Mrs. Cook and be sure the dog is all right.''

"I want to go with you,'' Mandie told him as she began removing her tam.

"I do, too,'' Celia said, taking off her coat.

"All right, girls, go ahead, but you'll have to hurry up to your room and get ready for supper. Make it quick now,'' Mrs. Hamilton told them.

Mrs. Yodkin came into the front hallway and overheard the conversation. "Yes, ma'am, the meal will be served at six since Mr. Guyer is not home. When he's here he prefers seven o'clock,'' she said.

"I hope you had a nice time. I will show you the way to your room if you'd like."

"Thank you, Mrs. Yodkin," Mrs. Hamilton replied. "I appreciate your offer, but I believe I know the way now." She smiled at the woman. "But I'd appreciate it if you would see that these girls get to their room as soon as they check on the dog."

"Yes, ma'am, that I will," Mrs. Yodkin replied as Mrs. Hamilton went into the hallway. "Young ladies, just hang your wraps on the hall tree if you please. And please hurry with your checking on the dog. I will wait here."

"Yes, ma'am, we'll be right back," Mandie told her as she and Celia hung up their coats and hats and quickly followed Jonathan down the hallway and into the kitchen.

When Jonathan pushed open the door to the kitchen, the white dog rushed forward and eagerly jumped around Jonathan. Mrs. Cook stood at the stove and turned to watch.

Jonathan told the girls, "You see how well trained he is. He must belong to someone who taught him not to jump all over your clothes." He reached down to pat the dog's head, and the dog immediately sat down. "Hello, fellow, you are a good doggie."

"He is a good dog, that he is," Mrs. Cook said. "Let me know every time he had to go out and then was ready to come right back inside. Stayed right here all day."

Mandie suddenly remembered her cat. "Oh, I forgot all about Snowball," she said. "He must be starved by now."

"No, no, miss," Mrs. Cook said. "I bring him down here. He eat everything I give him."

"You brought him down here? Where is he?" Mandie asked, glancing around the huge kitchen.

"I take him back to room," the woman said with a smile. "No worry. He's all right."

"Oh, thank you, Mrs. Cook," Mandie told her with a sigh of relief.

"Jonathan, I'm glad your dog is all right," Celia said. "But I think we'd better go upstairs to our room now."

"That girl came over the wall in the garden again, this afternoon it was," Mrs. Cook said. "When I tell her I will be calling for the police she goes away."

"So she did come back," Jonathan said.

"But she didn't come to knock on the door like you told her to," Mandie reminded him.

"Maybe I'd better look in the garden to be sure she's gone," Jonathan said, starting toward the door.

"I'll go with you," Mandie said as she followed.

"So will I," Celia added.

The three went out into the dark garden and looked around in the dim light. There was no sign of the girl, and Jonathan checked the gate to be sure it was locked.

Suddenly a chill ran over Mandie and she shivered. "Let's go back inside," she said. "I didn't realize it was so cold out here." She ran for the back door.

"We should have put our coats and hats back on," Celia said, racing after Mandie.

"This is only November, just the beginning of cold weather. You girls should come up during December and January. Then it's really cold," Jonathan told them as the three returned to the kitchen.

"Mandie, don't forget, Mrs. Yodkin is waiting for us," Celia reminded her as she started for the hallway.

"Oh, that's right," Mandie said. "Jonathan, we'll see you when we come back down for supper."

"I have to go to my room, too," Jonathan said.

The three left the kitchen, and Mrs. Yodkin showed the girls the way to their room even though Mandie insisted that she now knew the way.

All during the evening meal Mandie kept thinking it must be awfully cold, even with the furnace heat on and a fire crackling in the great fireplace in the dining room. She could hardly wait to get back to her room and crawl under the warm quilts on the big bed. The day had worn her out, and she was secretly wishing she was home in her own bed as everyone else carried on a conversation. New York was just too big and too busy for her.

Chapter 5 / Suspicious Happenings

The next morning Mandie woke up with a sore throat, and when she sat up in bed her nose began running. "Oh my goodness!" she exclaimed, reaching for her handkerchief on the table beside the bed.

"I was wondering if you were going to wake up in time for breakfast," Celia called to her from the bureau across the huge room, where she was brushing her long, curly auburn hair.

"Breakfast?" Mandie repeated as she pressed her hands against her aching head.

"What is it, Mandie? What's wrong?" Celia asked, quickly coming to stand beside the bed.

"Oh, shucks, Celia," Mandie said with an irritated sigh. "I do believe I'm getting a cold. Of all the unlucky things to happen to me!"

"I'm sorry, Mandie, but you do sound like it," Celia replied as she frowned.

Mandie swung her legs over the side of the big bed and said, "Maybe if I just get up and eat something it'll go away." She swallowed hard because her throat burned. "I just can't let this interfere with seeing New York."

"Yes, maybe you will feel better when you've dressed. I'll help you," Celia told her. "Which dress do you want to wear today? I'll get it from the wardrobe for you."

"Oh, anything that's warm will do. The navy wool one will be fine," Mandie said.

"Leila has already been in and built up the fire in the fireplace, and Zelda has brought the orange juice. It's on the tray over there," Celia told her, motioning across the room to a large table. Then she went over to the wardrobe to take down the dress Mandie wanted to wear.

With Celia's help, Mandie was dressed but feeling a little shaky by the time Mrs. Hamilton joined them to go down to breakfast. Zelda knocked on the door at about the same time.

"I'm sorry, but I seem to be getting a cold," Mandie told Mrs. Hamilton.

"Oh dear, maybe you should go back to bed and rest awhile longer," Mrs. Hamilton suggested.

"Eat first," Zelda said from the doorway. "Then rest."

Mandie tried hard to ignore the cold. She shut Snowball up in the bathroom, and they all went down to the dining room, where Jonathan was waiting for them at the door.

"My father rang up on the telephone last night to say he will be home this afternoon, Mrs. Hamilton," Jonathan told her as they entered the dining room.

"Thank you for letting me know, Jonathan," Mrs. Hamilton said. Everyone sat down at the table.

"Then I will go out and do some more shopping this morning." She glanced at Mandie and said, "Amanda, I think you had better stay inside today with that cold."

Mandie sighed loudly and asked, "Do I have to?"

"Yes, I think you have to. I am responsible for you right now, and I don't think you should go out in this cold weather," Mrs. Hamilton replied.

"If you don't need me to find your way around New York, Mrs. Hamilton, I'll stay here with Mandie, and Celia could go with you," Jonathan volunteered.

"Thank you, Jonathan. I'm sure your driver can find the stores where I want to shop," Mrs. Hamilton said with a smile.

"Mother, I could stay here with Mandie," Celia suggested.

"No, no. Amanda needs to get some rest, and besides, I may need you along to be fitted for clothes," her mother replied.

"I'm really not very interested in going shopping anyway, Celia, and I know you are, so y'all just go ahead," Mandie told her friend.

Once their breakfast was finished, Mrs. Hamilton and Celia left in the carriage. Mandie went with Jonathan to sit by the fire in the parlor.

"Before we get too comfortable here, I'd better take the dog outside for a few minutes," Jonathan told her as he stood up.

"Yes, we don't want any accidents," Mandie agreed with a smile. "And I'd better check on Snowball."

"Take him down to the kitchen where Mrs. Cook can feed him. She won't mind having him in there for a while. I'll bring the dog in here after he goes outside," Jonathan said.

Mandie rose, and the two started toward the hallway.

"Do you need me to show you the way back up to your room to get Snowball?" Jonathan asked.

"No, I think I can find the way now. But I must say, you sure do have a huge house," Mandie replied, smiling as they stepped into the corridor.

"My father keeps saying he is going to close off a lot of it except on special occasions, but he never gets around to doing that," Jonathan replied. "Now I go this way and you go that way. Please don't get lost." He motioned Mandie down the hallway to the right, and he went left.

"I won't," Mandie promised.

Mandie found the way to her room, rescued Snowball out of the bathroom, fastened on his leash, and started back downstairs.

"Now, don't get any frisky ideas," Mandie cautioned the cat as he tugged hard at the end of the leash.

But Snowball had a mind of his own. He suddenly jerked the leash out of Mandie's hand, raced down the stairs, and disappeared into the hallway.

"Snowball!" Mandie called. She ran after him. "Where are you? Kitty, kitty, come here." Her cold was getting worse, and she certainly didn't feel like chasing that cat. Looking into every room with an open door down the hallway, she came to the doorway to the glass room. The glass door was closed.

"I don't think Snowball could have opened this door," Mandie said to herself as she put her hand on the door and then stopped. The door seemed awfully easy to move. Snowball could have pushed his way into the glass room.

Mandie eased the door open just in case Snowball was on the other side. She knew she would have to sneak up in order to capture him. Cautiously moving into the room, she began searching the aisles between the plants. Finally she caught a glimpse of Snowball standing up on his hind legs in one of the huge pots, sharpening his claws on the thick trunk of the plant growing in it.

"Snow—" she started to call him as she moved in that direction, but she suddenly heard men's voices just beyond where she was standing.

Slipping between the large pots, Mandie was able to see the owners of the voices. Jens, the butler, and another man she had not seen before were standing just inside the door that opened out into the yard. She bent down and moved a little forward to get a better look. The stranger was tall, dark, middle-aged, and was wearing dark work clothes and a green beret. He looked foreign and seemed to be speaking a foreign language in a low voice.

Jens pulled an envelope out of his inside coat pocket, handed it to the man, and said, "Take this and don't let anyone know where you got it."

The man shrugged his shoulders, accepted the envelope, slipped it inside his jacket, and spoke again in a strange language.

Whatever the stranger was saying, Jens evidently disagreed with him. "No, no, no!" he interrupted the foreign man. "That is not the way it is done here. You must be patient. Haste will ruin everything."

Mandie's heart beat faster. These men sounded like they were planning something they shouldn't be doing. She couldn't understand a word the stranger was saying. Oh, if only Jonathan would come looking for her. He would probably be able to translate the man's conversation.

The scent of the wet soil in the pots suddenly tickled her nose and she sneezed loudly. She ducked down lower as she saw the two men look around. After what seemed like minutes, she finally heard Jens say, "I must go now."

The stranger mumbled something in his language.

Jens replied, "I will see you then. Remember, say nothing, not one word."

Jens quickly went out the door into the yard and the stranger followed. Mandie straightened up and quickly crept forward to look outside. The two men had vanished.

"Something strange is going on," Mandie mumbled to herself as she looked out into the yard. Something suddenly swished by her ankles and she jumped in fright. Looking down, she was relieved to see it was only Snowball. She quickly stepped on the end of his leash. Snowball meowed angrily as he tried to pull away.

"You are coming with me," she told him. She picked up the end of his leash and started toward the kitchen. This time she had no trouble finding her way.

"Ah, so here is that white cat," Mrs. Cook said as Mandie pushed open the door and stepped inside the kitchen. She put a lid on a pot on the stove and came toward Mandie. "Just you leave him here with me, and I will feed him."

"Has Jonathan been in here, Mrs. Cook?" Mandie asked as she stooped to unhook Snowball's leash.

"That he has, and he took the white dog to the little parlor," the woman told her. "Now, we will put this white cat behind this little door here, and I will know if he gets out," she continued, pointing toward a half-swinging door that closed off a counter at the back of the room.

Mandie picked up Snowball and took him across the room. "You know, Mrs. Cook, Snowball can jump over this door," she said while she looked at it. "Maybe I should leave his leash on him and fasten the other end to the catch on the door." She examined the hook holding the door in place.

"That will be fine," Mrs. Cook said as she went toward a storage cabinet back across the room. "You secure the white cat and I will get him food. Just leave him here with me. I will see that he does not get out."

Mandie looped the end of the leash around the door fastener while Snowball protested. "Thank you, Mrs. Cook," she said, straightening up. "Please don't let him get outside. I'll go find Jonathan now." She started toward the hall door.

"He will be here whenever you decide to return," Mrs. Cook promised.

"Thank you, Mrs. Cook," Mandie told her. She went out the door and into the hallway.

Mandie found her way back to the parlor. Jonathan was sitting by the fire, and the white dog was lying on the rug by the hearth. She sat down across from Jonathan and excitedly told him about Jens and the stranger.

Her throat hurt terribly bad, but she managed to give Jonathan all the details. "I think it was all awfully suspicious, the way they were acting and talking," she ended up.

Jonathan had sat still listening, and then he said, "I'm completely baffled. I can't imagine who the stranger was or what Jens was doing, giving an envelope to him and admonishing him to be secretive about it all." He frowned thoughtfully.

"I know we can't go ask Jens anything about all this, but we could keep a watch out in case anything else happens," Mandie said.

"But I don't see how we can even watch Jens without him knowing we are spying on him," Jonathan replied.

"Your father will be home this afternoon. Are you going to tell him about this? Maybe he could do something," Mandie told him.

"Yes, I suppose we should tell my father," Jonathan said, then he grinned. "But we'll feel really foolish if it turns out to be something my father knows about."

"But how could your father know anything about it?" Mandie asked.

"Oh, Mandie, that cold has slowed you down," Jonathan said, smiling. "Don't you remember my father does secret work for the government?"

"But, Jonathan, I thought he had quit all that. Remember, when we were in Europe you said he was getting out of it and would be staying home because he was allowing you to stay home to go to school here rather than those boarding schools all over the world where you'd been going," Mandie reminded him.

Jonathan laughed and said, "He did say that, and he did try to quit. But when President McKinley was assassinated and President Roosevelt was sworn into office, those people in Washington talked him into continuing his work for a while onger. He has cut back on the amount of time he works, though."

"So that is why he went to Washington yesterday," Mandie said. "But, Jonathan, exactly what does he do in Washington?"

Jonathan shrugged his shoulders and said, "I have no idea."

"But he's your father. You ought to know," Mandie said, looking at him in doubt as she stretched her feet toward the warmth of the fire.

"Mandie, that is the very reason he doesn't tell me anything," Jonathan protested. "That way he can be sure I don't go around telling things I ought not to. Besides, if somebody managed to kidnap me, they wouldn't be able to get any information from me."

"Kidnapped? Oh, Jonathan, the very word scares me," Mandie said. "I think you'd better tell your father about Jens and the strange man. I just feel like something is going on, and if your father knows what it is, then that's all right, but if he doesn't, then he should be made aware of it."

"Of course, you're absolutely right, Mandie," Jonathan agreed. "As soon as he gets home I'll talk to him, without anyone else hearing about it, just in case it is something he is aware of, something that should be kept a secret."

"I won't mention it to anyone else," Mandie promised. "Maybe your father will return before Celia and her mother get back, and you'll have a chance to talk then."

Jonathan shifted in his chair and said, "Now that that's all settled, what do you say we do? Just sit here so you can rest? Or do you feel like playing a game of chess or something?"

"I feel better than I did when I first got up," Mandie replied. "I just can't talk too well because of my sore throat. But I'd say I'm up to whatever you'd like to do."

"Well, what will it be?" Jonathan asked.

"I'm not much of a chess player. Uncle John taught me, and he says I talk too much," Mandie said, laughing.

"Mrs. Hamilton didn't want you to go shopping with her and Celia because of your cold, but do you suppose it will be all right if we just walked out in the garden?" Jonathan asked.

"That's a good idea. I need some fresh air," Mandie said, rising from her chair. "And I don't think it would hurt my cold at all. I'll get my coat and hat."

"And I'll get mine," Jonathan said, standing up. As Mandie started toward the hallway, he added, "And I believe Zelda took your coat and hat up to your room. She's always clearing things off the hall tree. I know she put mine in my room." He followed her into the hallway.

"That's all right," Mandie said. "I'll run upstairs and get it."

"The maids are all working upstairs right now, so if you don't find it, you can ask one of them," Jonathan told her. "I'll meet you back here."

"Right," Mandie agreed as she went one way and Jonathan the other.

When she reached the top of the staircase, she could hear the maids talking in nearby rooms while they worked. She hurried to the room she shared with Celia and was glad to find her coat and hat hanging in the huge wardrobe.

"Thank goodness I don't have to hunt for it," she

said to herself as she stood before a long mirror and slipped into her warm coat and hastily pulled her tam over her blond hair. Reaching into her pocket as she started for the door, she pulled out her gloves and began putting them on as she hurried back to the parlor.

"I'm ready," she said, rushing into the room. She stopped and looked around. Jonathan had not returned, but the white dog raised his head by the fireplace to watch her. "And I suppose you want to go, too," she said to him.

Behind her, Jonathan had come into the room and said, "Let's leave him here. I've already had him out, remember?"

"Oh yes, and I left Snowball in the kitchen so I don't have to take him outside," Mandie said.

"Then let's go," Jonathan told her.

As they passed the kitchen door, Mandie stopped and said, "Let me just check on Snowball to be sure he is still here."

Jonathan reached from behind her and pushed the door open. Mandie almost stepped on the butler lying on the floor, all tied up with ropes around his legs and his hands and a gag in his mouth. Snowball was roaming around the room.

"Jens!" Jonathan exclaimed, rushing to the butler to untie the ropes and remove the rag from his mouth. "What happened? What happened?"

As soon as the butler could speak, he said, "Thief! Stole—"

"Jonathan, there they are!" Mandie cried, glimpsing someone running down the hallway. She ran into the hallway in pursuit.

Leaving the butler with his feet still tied up, Jonathan rushed after her. "The girl!" he exclaimed as the figure disappeared down the hallway.

"And that man!" Mandie added, spotting the strange man who had been talking to Jens. He was following the girl.

The two young people chased after the girl and the strange man and saw them escape through the back door.

"Hurry!" Mandie cried to Jonathan, racing ahead through the open door.

"The cat!" Jonathan called to her as Snowball quickly followed his mistress outside.

Mandie glanced down, saw her cat, quickly scooped him up into her arms, and kept running through the garden. Jonathan caught up with her.

"There they go," Jonathan said, pointing down the street as he and Mandie went out through the garden's open gate.

"He went that way," Mandie said, slowing down when she saw the man go down an alley to the left.

"And the girl went that way," Jonathan said.

Mandie could see her still running down the street in the opposite direction. "Let's go after her," she told Jonathan.

They had narrowed the gap with the girl when she suddenly ran into a small second-hand shop. Jonathan paused, but Mandie looked back and said, "Come on. She'll get away."

Jonathan caught up with Mandie, and together they entered the shop and looked around. An old man sat behind a small counter at the back of what looked like a used clothing store. There was no one else in sight.

"Did a girl come in here just now?" Mandie quickly asked him.

The man looked at her but gave no evidence of

understanding what she was saying.

"A girl? About ten years old? Not quite as tall as I am?" Mandie continued with her questions while Snowball squirmed in her arms.

The man just looked at her and then at Jonathan.

"I think he is deaf, Mandie," Jonathan said in a whisper.

Mandie looked at the man and decided Jonathan was correct. She began looking among the piles of clothing and narrow aisles but could find no trace of the girl.

"I don't think she is in here," Jonathan said as he, too, thoroughly examined the contents of the store.

"Let's go back and see if we can find out where the man went," Mandie suggested.

"He's probably long gone by now," Jonathan said.

"He might not be. Maybe he saw us go after the girl and decided we weren't going to chase him, so he could be somewhere near where we saw him," Mandie replied. "Come on."

"All right, but I think you're wasting your time," Jonathan reluctantly agreed.

"We won't know until we go look," Mandie said.

The two young people went out of the store and hurried back in the direction they had come.

Chapter 6 / On the Run!

"Jonathan, that man who was in your house was the same man I saw talking to the butler this morning," Mandie managed to tell Jonathan as they ran. She was nearly out of breath.

"Why didn't you tell me so? I would have chased him instead of the girl," Jonathan replied, slowing down so Mandie could keep up with him.

"Sorry—everything was—so fast," Mandie said between gasps.

When they got to the place where the man had disappeared, they stopped to consider what they should do next. They stood looking down the dark alley where the man had vanished.

"I believe this alley has nothing in it but the back doors of all the shops along the street around the corner," Jonathan said.

"And he could have gone into any of the shops," Mandie added.

"I just thought of something. When you told me

about seeing him in our house this morning, you said he was speaking a foreign language. If I only knew what language it was, we could look in the neighborhood where that nationality of people live," Jonathan said.

"You mean there's a whole neighborhood full of foreign-speaking people?" Mandie asked in surprise.

"Oh, there are lots of languages spoken here in New York, and the people of each different language live in clusters," he explained. "So if I knew his language, I could locate the settlement of his kind of people."

"I'm sorry, Jonathan, but I don't believe I have ever heard such a language before. Of course, we don't have any foreign-speaking people down in North Carolina where I come from, and I haven't heard any other languages except when we went to Europe this past summer," Mandie told him. Snowball squirmed in her arms.

"I'd like to know how they got into the house and managed to tie Jens up," Jonathan said as he continued scanning up and down the streets at the intersection.

"And I wonder what they stole. Your butler was saying, 'Thieves,' and was trying to tell us what they had taken," Mandie reminded him, still peering down the dark alleyway. "I didn't see Mrs. Cook in the kitchen, either. She had promised to watch out for Snowball."

"Well, are we going down through there or not?" Jonathan asked with a big grin. "We could at least check around the doorways."

"Of course," Mandie agreed. "Let's go."

The two young people cautiously entered the

alley and began slowly inspecting the back doors of the shops. Almost all of the businesses had trash cans beside the entrances. Here and there they found a window, but the glass was always barred and too dirty to see through.

"It's awfully dark in here for it to be daylight outside," Mandie remarked.

"That's because it's cloudy and also because the buildings are so close together. Everything in New York is crammed in," Jonathan said while he examined a dark recess at the corner of a building.

Snowball suddenly growled and almost jumped out of Mandie's arms. She quickly squeezed him tight. "Snowball, be still," she told him. But the white cat struggled to get free.

"Watch out!" Jonathan suddenly called to her.

Mandie looked toward the corner where he was standing and saw something rushing toward her. Snowball growled angrily and fought with her to get down.

"What is it?" She gasped as she tried to catch her breath.

The flying object dashed past her, and as it disappeared down the alley she realized it was another cat. Then out of nowhere a dog materialized and chased after the animal.

"Whew!" Mandie said, letting out a deep breath.

Jonathan walked back to where she was standing. "Are you all right?" he asked. "Those animals were in the trash cans."

"Yes, I'm all right, but let's hurry and finish looking through this dark place," Mandie said, rubbing Snowball's head to calm him down. She put her handkerchief to her nose when she smelled the rotting garbage that the animals had stirred up.

Mandie stayed close to Jonathan the rest of the way, and they finally came out onto the street at the end. They had not met up with anyone in the alley.

"Now I suppose we should look in the front doors of all the shops," Jonathan suggested.

"Maybe if we described the man someone might have seen him," Mandie said as they walked up to the door of the first shop on the block.

"We can try that if you can remember what the man looked like," Jonathan replied. "I was so busy untying Jens I didn't get a good look at him. I would recognize the girl, but I don't know about the man."

"He was tall, dark-looking," Mandie began as they stopped for a moment. "He had on everyday clothes, like a man would work in, dark grayish, and the main thing I noticed was that he was wearing a green beret."

"A green beret?" Jonathan asked thoughtfully. "Could the man have been French?"

"I may be wrong, but it didn't sound like French he was speaking," Mandie replied. "Not the kind of French we heard when we were in France."

"Was it a slower language? You know the French talk rather fast sometimes," Jonathan told her.

"No, it was fast, all jumbled together in fact," Mandie replied. "And he must have been able to understand English because Jens was speaking English. I understood that much when Jens gave him that envelope and then told him not to let anyone know where he got it, and that haste would ruin everything, and all that."

Jonathan thought for a moment and said, "Then Jens must have been able to understand the man's language, too, and I'm just not sure how many languages Jens knows. I do know he has a good education. My father hired him away from the household of an earl in England where he was working. Jens wanted to come to the United States and had not been able to because of money."

"Those people in England seemed to know so many languages when we visited there, like German, French, and some I never figured out," Mandie replied. Snowball had finally calmed down and clung to the shoulder of her coat.

"On your trip there is one language I don't think you ran into, and that is Spanish," Jonathan said, suddenly brightening up. "They also talk with their hands. Did this man use his hands when he talked?"

Mandie frowned and thought about that. "Why, yes, I believe he did," she said. "He talked real fast, and I remember his hands sort of accenting the words he was saying."

"Aha! Let's try a Spanish neighborhood," Jonathan decided. "I know where there are several hundred tenements that Spanish people live in."

"Several hundred?" Mandie asked. "Jonathan, how will we ever find anybody in a place that big?"

"We'll just walk around and look and ask questions," Jonathan said. "Come on. It's within walking distance if you feel up to it. How's your cold?" He smiled at her.

"My cold is a nuisance more than anything," Mandie said. "But aren't we even going to look in all these shops around here? The man did go this way."

"You're right," Jonathan agreed. "Let's start here at the corner and work our way down the block. This is a mixed area—a Jewish delicatessen, a German butcher, a Dutch candy store, a Negro shoe shine parlor, a Chinese laundry, and lots more.

I've been down this street before."

The two young people began entering the shops, looking around, and going on to the next one. Jonathan asked several store owners if they had seen such a man as he described but without any luck.

Then as they entered the last shop, which was a soda shop on a corner, Mandie looked ahead through the store and spotted the stranger. He looked directly at her, then turned and ran out the back door.

"Jonathan, there he is!" Mandie yelled as she tightened her hold on the white cat and chased after the man.

Mandie reached the back door first and shoved it open. Jonathan caught up with her and together they came out into the same back alley they had gone down earlier.

"He's disappeared," Mandie said in a disappointed voice, scanning the dark alleyway. She stomped her foot and added, "Oh, shucks! He was right there in that store, and now he got away."

"Come on. We'll find him again," Jonathan told her. "He couldn't have gotten very far away."

They began searching the passageway and watching to see if any of the doors were open. Finally coming to the corner and out into the street, the two stopped to look around.

"He sure disappeared fast," Mandie remarked.

"But I imagine he is still in the neighborhood," Jonathan added. "Let's look in the shops again. More than likely he stepped inside a store."

"He really must be guilty of something to run from us that way," Mandie said.

"Sure he is," Jonathan told her. "Remember

Jens was calling the man and the girl thieves, and he said they had stolen something. So I am pretty sure he has committed a crime of some kind."

Mandie reached to touch Jonathan's arm. "Jonathan, we should be awfully careful. He could be dangerous if he's committed a crime," she reminded him.

Jonathan patted her hand and said, "Just don't get out of my sight."

"But, Jonathan, if we do finally get him to stop running away, or I should say, catch up with him, what are we going to do? We can't arrest him," Mandie said.

"No, but we can make such a fuss that everyone within listening distance will stop to see what's going on," Jonathan said. "Besides, there are quite a few policemen walking the beat around here. We might be lucky enough to see one."

At that moment something touched Mandie's nose, and she looked up to see light snowflakes beginning to fall. "Jonathan, it's snowing!" she exclaimed as she cuddled Snowball closer.

Jonathan looked upward also and said, "Just a few flakes here and there. It may not even really snow. But, anyway, we're wasting time. Let's go through all these stores again."

"If I see him again, I'll try to dodge out of his sight and signal to you so we can trip him or something before he knows we're around," Mandie said as they stepped up to the door of the corner shop.

They walked in and out of several stores, looking over the people inside, but had no luck until they came to the Chinese laundry.

As they stepped inside, Mandie laid her hand on Jonathan's arm to stop him. "That man behind the counter," she whispered. "I think that's the man. He's taken off his green beret."

Jonathan glanced at her and then walked toward the man with Mandie close behind him. When they reached the counter, the man saw them and suddenly shoved down a lever that blew up a cloud of steam, blinding their view.

Mandie wiped her face and cried, "I can't see a thing, Jonathan!"

Jonathan, by her side, blew out his breath and said, "I can see enough to know he grabbed his green beret from the shelf under the counter, put it on his head, and disappeared in the fog."

Mandie looked toward the front door. The air was clear in that direction, and she had not seen the man go that way. "He went out the back door," she said. "Come on."

The two rushed past the Chinaman working on a laundry press and out the back door. This time they were in luck. The man was still in sight as he ran down the dark alley.

"Let's go," Mandie said, reaching for Jonathan's hand and holding on to Snowball with her other arm.

The two raced down the alley in pursuit. When they came to the end, they saw the man run across the street and disappear behind some bushes in a small park. They kept right on running after him.

Jonathan suddenly yelled something in a foreign language, and Mandie looked at him as he waved ahead.

"What are you saying?" she managed to ask as she began gasping for breath. She felt like the cold was really stuffing up her lungs.

"I asked him to wait so we could talk to him, in

Spanish, that is," Jonathan explained as they slowed down to examine the area around the bushes where the man had gone.

"He sure can disappear fast," Mandie said. "That's all I can think about. How fast he can run."

"He knows by now that we are really in earnest about catching up with him, so he has to run all the faster," Jonathan said, looking behind a bench.

Mandie happened to glance ahead and saw the green beret moving past a sign at the far end of the little park. "Look!" she exclaimed and pointed in that direction. "There he is!"

Mandie and Jonathan kept chasing the man, but he kept outrunning them. He led them through various kinds of neighborhoods and business districts but didn't seem able to completely disappear.

Mandie's side was hurting, and Snowball was heavy to carry while running. Her throat got sorer and sorer, but she didn't complain. She did her dead-level best to keep up with Jonathan, who didn't seem to tire at all.

Then suddenly Mandie thought the world was tumbling. There was a terrific roar all around her, and she looked up to see train cars running on a platform far above the street. She had never even heard of such a thing, much less seen it. She stopped in amazement, and Jonathan happened to look back and saw that she had stopped.

"Come on!" he called out above the noise, stepping back to take her hand. "That's just the elevated railroad up there. Come on."

Mandie allowed him to pull her forward as she continued to stare at the miracle above, trains running up in the air!

"I see him over there behind that building with

the horse tied up in front," Jonathan told Mandie, still pulling her along with him.

Mandie quickly looked where he was pointing. The man, still wearing the green beret, was sitting on the doorstep of the tenement house where the horse stood. Evidently he had not seen them.

"Maybe we can catch up with him now," she said eagerly as the two of them ran across the cobblestone street, dodging between drays pulled by horses and children playing in the street.

Just as the two got to the other side of the street, the man finally saw them. He jumped up and ran up the stairs to the overhead railroad.

"Come on," Jonathan urged Mandie as he started after the man.

Mandie got to the stairs and then suddenly pulled her hand out of Jonathan's. "We can't go up there. That train may come back and run over us," she cried.

"Oh, come on, Mandie," Jonathan coaxed her. "There's more than one track up there. We can get out of the way if it comes back. Come on. I'll show you."

"I can't walk up in the air like that," Mandie insisted, nervously holding on to Snowball.

"Mandie, the man is getting away. After all the time we've spent chasing him, let's not quit now or we'll never find him again," Jonathan insisted. "Please!"

Mandie looked at Jonathan, took a deep breath, and said, "Only if you will hold my hand and catch me if I start to fall."

Jonathan grinned at her and said, "I'll hold your hand anytime, Mandie Shaw, and I sure won't let you fall. Now come on." He reached for her free hand.

Clinging to Jonathan on one side and squeezing her cat with her other arm, Mandie managed to climb the steps to the railroad tracks.

"You have to be careful to walk on the edge where the train doesn't run because the tracks actually have electricity to make the train move," Jonathan explained as he led her down the narrow walkway.

Mandie stopped and said, "Electricity? Jonathan, we could be—what do you call it—electrocuted? This is dangerous!"

Jonathan grinned and said, "No danger of that if you just do what I tell you. And for goodness' sakes, Mandie, please don't let that cat get away from you."

Mandie finally smiled at him and said, "Jonathan, you live a dangerous life, playing around with trains and electricity."

"Come on," Jonathan said, looking down the track. "We may have lost the man unless we can see him when we go around this curve."

Mandie practically held her breath as she allowed Jonathan to lead her down the pathway next to the tracks. She was so nervous she had to watch her footsteps and left it to Jonathan to spot the man.

As they came around the curve in the tracks, Jonathan suddenly exclaimed, "There he goes! And I don't believe he knows we are behind him." He quickened his footsteps, and Mandie took a deep breath and followed.

After what seemed like hours to Mandie, they finally came to a train stop where there was a waiting place for passengers. However, it was on the opposite side of the tracks from where they were walk-ing.

"We have to cross the tracks now, Mandie," Jonathan told her. "The man went over there and down to the street."

Mandie looked down at the dangerous tracks, contemplating how she would be able to get to the other side. Suddenly there was a loud commotion and the tracks began to shake under her feet. Jonathan quickly put his arm around her and screamed above the noise, "No problem. Just a train coming down the other side. Stand very still."

Mandie's heart did flip-flops as the train came rumbling down the tracks and then stopped on the other side from where they were standing. She was shaking so hard she could hardly stand up, what with the train also shaking the very rails under her feet.

Then suddenly the train started to move on down the tracks, and the vibration finally stopped.

"Now," Jonathan told her. "Here. I'll take Snowball to the other side." He took the white cat in one arm and reached for Mandie's hand. "Hold on to me."

Mandie looked down at her feet again and realized her long skirts were in the way. She lifted up the garments and held them tightly in her other hand as Jonathan guided her across the tracks.

"Whew!" Mandie exclaimed with a loud sigh, al-most collapsing with relief after they managed to get back down to the street.

"Come on, Mandie," Jonathan urged her. "That man went this way. Maybe we can get a glimpse of him somewhere. Help me watch for him." He looked down at her and grinned. "Now you can go home and tell everybody you walked down the elevated railroad tracks in New York."

"Never," Mandie said. "My mother would have a heart attack." She allowed Jonathan to lead her down the street as she took Snowball back into her arms. She rubbed his fur and talked to him, "Poor kitty, you were scared, too."

"Do I hear Mandie Shaw admitting she was scared? Never have I heard that she was scared by anything," Jonathan teased as they rushed down the street.

"You are not playing fair, Jonathan," Mandie objected. "You are used to this crazy life in New York, and I've never been here before. And I've certainly never been on overhead railroad tracks before. Just you wait till you come to visit us in North Carolina. I'll get even with you on some things, too."

Jonathan glanced at her, smiled, and then looked ahead. "There! That man is going into that tenement building over there. Hurry! We'll go inside and follow him."

Go inside a tenement building? Mandie thought. *What's inside there?* New York was a strange place to her. She didn't mind chasing strangers out in the open streets, but to enter a strange building! That could be dangerous.

Jonathan gave her hand a pull and said, "Come on, Mandie, we're wasting time. He'll get away again."

"I'll sure be glad when we do catch up with him," Mandie replied as she reluctantly followed.

Chapter 7 / A Strange Neighborhood

Even with her cold, Mandie could smell the strong odor of garlic in food cooking somewhere in the tenement building as she and Jonathan stepped inside the front hallway. The front door had been closed but was unlocked. A draft in the hallway indicated something was open beyond as the wind practically whistled through. She shivered with cold and fright. Snowball meowed loudly in her arms.

Jonathan held her hand as they paused near the front door. Mandie stepped closer to him. She could hear loud voices intermingled with even louder quarreling and children yelling from somewhere inside the building.

"Now what?" she whispered.

"Let's look around," Jonathan whispered back, holding her hand as they walked down the long hallway.

Several doors along the way stood half-open with different noises coming out from behind them.

Some doors were closed. Mandie counted at least eight doors before they suddenly came to the back door. It stood wide open, hanging halfway off its hinges. The wind bellowed through it into the building.

Mandie shivered and held Snowball closer. *What a terrible place to live*, she thought. *What kind of people inhabit this rundown building?*

"What a horrible place to live," Jonathan echoed her thoughts in a low voice. "Let's go back to the front."

Just as they came to the back side of the staircase, they both saw the strange man going up the steps. They quickly followed, but the man had a good start and disappeared before they could see where he went.

"Let's go up to the top and we can search our way down," Jonathan suggested.

The old staircase creaked, and the loose spindles in the banister rattled under their combined weight and the strong draft of air from below. Mandie would not have been surprised if the whole thing had collapsed at any moment.

"Let's get off these steps," she whispered to Jonathan when they finally reached the top floor.

Stepping into the hallway, Jonathan went toward a door straight ahead and said, "All right, but first let's look on the roof and see if he went there."

Jonathan pushed the door open, revealing a short staircase that he quickly climbed. Mandie followed, but as she stepped through the doorway, Snowball suddenly managed to jump out of her arms. He ran back into the hallway. The door slammed shut with Mandie on one side and Snowball on the other. She frantically pulled on the door but couldn't get it to open.

"What are you doing?" Jonathan called down to her.

"The door shut and Snowball is in there. I can't get the door open!" she cried out in panic.

Jonathan rushed down and helped her pull on the door, but without any results.

"The door must have locked when it slammed shut," Jonathan told her in dismay, looking helplessly about.

"What are we going to do, Jonathan?" Mandie exclaimed. "Snowball will run off and I'll never find him! Oh, Jonathan, we've got to do something."

"We'll just have to wait until somebody comes up here," he said. "I need to search the roof, Mandie, to see if the man is out there. Come on. Maybe someone will help us."

Mandie followed Jonathan up the short staircase and realized they were completely outside the building. The door had closed off the tenement house behind them, and now they were out on the open roof.

Jonathan reached for her hand and said, "Come on. Let's walk around the chimney so we can see what's up here."

After they passed the chimney, Mandie could see there was nothing else on the roof, and when she looked over the edge she could see for blocks and blocks around. The sudden realization that they were on top of a building without any rails or protection around the outer edges made Mandie slightly dizzy. Her hold tightened on Jonathan's hand.

"What's wrong?" Jonathan asked, looking at her in concern.

"I—I—just never—have been this high up without something to keep me from falling over the edge," Mandie managed to say in a squeaky voice.

"You have me," Jonathan told her. "I won't let you fall over the edge. Besides, once you get used to being up here and looking down there on everything, you'll get over the fright."

A gust of wind blew across the roof, and Mandie pulled her coat collar up, trying not to shiver. She glanced up at the cloudy sky and asked, "What will we do if it snows, Jonathan?"

"I don't think it will snow. Besides, I don't expect to stay up here long. Someone must have seen us and will probably come to see what we're doing," he said. "Not only that, your cat will be found by someone down there, and then they will surely come looking for you."

"But, Jonathan, no one saw us come up here," Mandie reminded him.

"That's what you think. The kind of people who live in a building like this know and see everything that goes on," Jonathan said as they stood together in the middle of the roof.

"If we didn't see them, how could they see us?" Mandie asked. "I don't believe you, Jonathan Guyer. You're just trying to keep me from being worried."

"Mandie, remember all those half-open doors? And all those noises in the house?" Jonathan replied. "Well, those people who were making those noises were also peeking through the cracks to see what we were doing. I felt it."

"Then I wish they would hurry up and come to the roof," Mandie said. "In fact, I think we should just go back down those steps and beat and bang on that door and scream and holler until someone hears us."

"Remember, this is New York, Mandie. That might work in other places, but no one in New York is curious about someone beating and banging and screaming and hollering," Jonathan said. "Sooner or later someone will come up here."

"Suppose that man we've been following comes up here. Won't you be afraid of him way up here on this roof by ourselves?" Mandie asked.

"No, because there are two of us and only one of him," Jonathan replied with a big grin.

"But he must have friends, or even family, in this building because he did come in here while we watched him? He could bring the whole kit and caboodle right up here," Mandie argued. She looked around the roof and added, "Oh, how did we ever do such a dumb thing, getting locked out on the roof of a ramshackle old building like this?"

"Because we were in such a hurry," Jonathan replied. "We had to hurry or lose sight of the man. And I don't even know what he and the girl might have stolen from my father's house. It could have been something very valuable."

"And you know that no one at your house even knows where we are," Mandie reminded him. "If we don't get back there soon, Celia's mother will go absolutely wild when she finds we ran off and haven't returned."

"I know. I've been thinking about that, but right now there is nothing we can do about it except just wait for someone to open that door," Jonathan reminded her.

"Do you suppose we could attract someone's

attention down on the street if we yelled and waved?" Mandie asked.

"We can try," Jonathan replied. "Do you think you can walk to the edge of the roof without getting tipsy?" He grinned at her.

"Of course," Mandie tried to answer in a firm voice, but secretly her head began to swim just thinking of looking over the edge of the roof.

"Come on, then," Jonathan said, starting forward and holding her hand.

"Slowly, Jonathan, don't go too fast," Mandie cautioned him and then looked up with a big smile. "Or we might just not be able to stop and step right off into space."

Suddenly she heard a noise coming from below the steps they had climbed to the roof, and before she could speak, Jonathan said, "I hear someone. Come on!"

The two rushed back down to the locked door, listened for the noise, and when they heard it again they began pounding on the door.

"Please open the door," Jonathan called loudly between blows.

"We're locked out," Mandie cried as loudly as her sore throat would allow.

When the two stopped to listen, everything was silent on the other side of the door. Then they began again, beating and kicking the door. They heard the noise on the other side again, but when they stopped making their noises, whatever was inside also stopped.

"They must hear us," Mandie complained.

"It sounds like someone is in the hallway on the other side of this door," Jonathan said. "So the must know we're out here and just don't want to let us back in."

Mandie looked at him with worried eyes. "You mean that strange man may be leaving us out here to get rid of us because we followed him?" she asked.

"Could be," Jonathan agreed.

After a while they no longer heard anything inside the house, and Jonathan said, "Let's try your suggestion. We'll go back up on the roof and see if someone down on the street will hear us."

Mandie followed him up and out onto the roof. She held tightly to his hand as they slowly walked to the edge. Halfway across, she pulled him to a stop and said, "Jonathan, I think we ought to say our verse."

"Our verse? What verse?" he asked, puzzled by the question.

"Remember all those escapades we got into in Europe? We always say my favorite verse when we're afraid. Remember?" Mandie asked, looking up at him.

"Oh yes, I remember. I had forgotten about it, or I should say I haven't had the right occasion to say it," Jonathan told her.

"Now is the right time," Mandie said, holding his hand tightly and looking toward the cloudy sky. "Ready?"

"Ready," Jonathan agreed.

Together they recited Mandie's favorite verse. " 'What time I am afraid, I will put my trust in thee.' "

"Now I'm not afraid to look down at the street," Mandie said, still holding Jonathan's hand as they advanced to the edge of the roof.

Peering down to the street, for a moment everything did swim around in Mandie's head, and then things straightened up when she took a deep breath. People were walking on the sidewalk below, and she felt that it must be possible to get help from someone.

"Hello, down there!" she yelled as loudly as she could and waved her arms.

"Hey, you, down there!" Jonathan called out.

No one seemed to hear them even though they stood there yelling and waving for a few minutes. Mandie almost lost her voice and had to stop, and Jonathan decided to rest.

"That's New York for you. No one pays attention to anyone else," he complained.

"I think I'll sit down a minute," Mandie said, practically collapsing onto the roof. She was just far enough from the edge so she couldn't see over it.

"Good idea," Jonathan agreed as he sat down next to her.

"I wonder what time it is," Mandie said.

"Sorry, but I didn't wear my watch. I'd guess it's around noontime," he replied. "You can't tell by the sun because of the clouds, but my stomach is beginning to tell me that it's time to eat. All that food they're cooking in this building makes me hungry, even though it does smell to high heaven with all that seasoning."

"If you think it's only noontime, maybe we'll be able to get down from here and back to your house before Celia and her mother return from shopping," Mandie said in a cracked voice. She felt hot, then felt ice cold. She was just plain miserable with the cold, but she would never let Jonathan know.

"I sure hope so," Jonathan replied.

"And, Jonathan, I almost forgot about Snowball," Mandie told him. "I don't know where he is, and if we can ever get down from here, I'll have to find him before I can go back to your house."

"He's probably downstairs somewhere looking for that food the people in this house are cooking," Jonathan said with a laugh. "We don't know now where that man is that we were chasing."

"He's probably the one who closed that door and locked it behind us," Mandie said.

"Maybe, but most of the houses in New York have an automatic lock on the doors to the roofs. When you close them, they lock unless you release the catch on the inside before you go out. And I—"

"And you forgot to do it," Mandie interrupted. "Oh, Jonathan, how could you forget such an important thing?"

"I'm sorry, Mandie. I really and truly am," Jonathan said. "But I still think someone in this house will come to see what we are doing up here."

"Jonathan, do you have any idea what that man and girl might have stolen from your house?" Mandie asked. "It must have been small because I don't remember seeing them carrying anything when they ran away."

"I would say the girl was after the dog, but she sure didn't have him when we saw her leave," Jonathan said thoughtfully. "Maybe we surprised them and they weren't able to take anything."

"But your butler said they stole something. He knew what it was, I suppose," Mandie said. "From the way things are going, whatever it was, we'll never be able to recover it."

"Ah, now, Mandie, don't give up hope," Jonathan said, reaching over to pull a strand of blond hair that had escaped from her hat.

Mandie pulled her hair out of his fingers and gave him a hard shove. "Jonathan, please behave," she said. "This is a serious situation we've got ourselves into, and I don't know how we're ever going to get out."

"I'm sorry, Mandie," he said, straightening up. "I suppose I'm really worried silly and don't want to admit it."

"Let's go back and bang on the door again," Mandie said, getting to her feet.

"All right," Jonathan agreed as he, too, stood up. "Never can tell. Someone might come and open it."

They went back down the short staircase and began beating on the door again and yelling and stomping their feet. When they finally paused for breath, Mandie thought she heard something on the other side.

"Did you hear that?" she asked.

"What?" Jonathan asked.

"I thought I heard someone close another door inside the house," she explained.

Jonathan listened for a moment and said, "No, I didn't hear a thing. Maybe I was making too much noise myself to hear it."

They waited at the door for a few minutes but didn't hear another sound inside.

"Let's go back on the roof and see if we can attract someone's attention down on the street," Jonathan said.

"All right, but you will have to do most of the yelling because I am losing my voice from this cold," Mandie said, trying to clear her throat.

"I'm sorry you're sick, Mandie. I know you

ought not be out here in this cold wind," Jonathan said as they climbed back up on the roof and walked over to the edge.

Mandie held on to Jonathan's hand and closed her eyes. The height really did make her dizzy. She cautiously opened her eyes and looked over the edge. The clotheslines were still down there, the laundry was still on them, and people were still rushing along the street, so she was sure it must all be real. She sank down on her knees with Jonathan and dared to look down again.

"Mandie, look—" Jonathan started to say.

"Jonathan!" Mandie interrupted, anxiously gazing below. "There is Snowball, on that windowsill. Oh, Jonathan, he might fall off."

"Are you sure it's Snowball?" Jonathan asked as he tried to see down below them.

"I know it's Snowball, and if I call to him he really will fall off," Mandie said with tears in her blue eyes. "What am I going to do?" She kept staring below, forgetting all about her fear of the height.

"He will probably just go back inside," Jonathan told her as he kept watching the cat below.

And at that moment Snowball did disappear back through the window.

"Oh, thank goodness, he did," Mandie said with a big sigh of relief. She looked at Jonathan and asked, "How did you know he would do that?"

"Oh, I was just guessing," Jonathan said. "I know most cats are afraid of heights and that if he looked down he would back up into the house."

"You're right, but he's not a normal cat and sometimes he doesn't act like a cat should," Mandie said with a nervous laugh. "Now I wonder where he is, where that window goes. Someone may see him and try to take him."

"I think they'll put him down awfully fast, too, because that cat knows how to scratch if he doesn't like what you do to him," Jonathan told her with a grin.

"You're right again," Mandie agreed. A strong gust of icy wind made her shiver through and through. She pulled her coat around her legs and started to get up.

"Moving back from the edge?" Jonathan asked as he stood up and offered his hand.

"It's so cold up here," Mandie said. She took one last look below and almost lost her breath. Snowball was in the window below again and his front paw was testing the clothesline strung across to the window in the opposite building. "Snowball!" she whispered.

Jonathan quickly joined her to see what was happening. He looked down and then at Mandie. "I'm sorry, Mandie," he said. "There's nothing we can do."

"Snowball, please, please go back inside," Mandie whispered to herself.

Jonathan sat back down beside her. "I can't yell down to the street because that might distract your cat, but maybe I could wave and someone will see me. What do you think?" Jonathan asked.

"Yes, please don't make any sound that would cause Snowball to look up or he might fall," Mandie said, continuing to watch the white cat who had now backed up onto the windowsill.

Jonathan leaned over and began waving his hat at the people below, but no one seemed to notice.

"Maybe if I drop my hat someone will see it," Jonathan suggested.

"Oh, no, Jonathan, you'd freeze to death without your hat. There's no telling how much longer we'll have to stay here on this roof," Mandie replied. She watched Snowball below as he finally sat down on the windowsill.

"Maybe I ought to go back to the door and beat on it some more," Jonathan suggested. "It wouldn't hurt anything to keep trying." He stood up again.

"All right, Jonathan, but please don't be too long," Mandie told him.

"I'll be right back," he promised and walked back across the roof.

Mandie kept watching her cat below. Snowball was evidently satisfied with the windowsill and lay down and curled up to sleep. Mandie breathed a sigh of relief. If he would only sleep awhile, maybe they would soon be able to get down from the roof and rescue him.

Then she had another thought. How would she ever find that particular window in the building in order to get Snowball? Someone must be living in the room where it was, and the house seemed full of people.

But somehow she would have to find her cat.

Chapter 8 / Out of Commission

After what seemed like hours and hours on the roof, Mandie became so miserable with her cold she didn't even want to talk any more. She could see that Jonathan was worried and had run out of anything to say. They sat safely back from the edge of the roof, and Mandie only moved to check on Snowball now and then. He was still asleep on the windowsill.

Suddenly there was a loud noise at the door below, and both of them rushed down the short staircase to see what it was.

"Look, the door is opening!" Jonathan exclaimed, running ahead to see who was doing this.

"Thank the Lord!" Mandie managed to say as she followed.

When the door came open far enough to see inside the hallway, Mandie saw the girl who had claimed the white dog, peeking out at them.

"We're glad you came—" Jonathan began as he got to the door.

"Stop!" the girl interrupted as she started to slam the door shut.

Jonathan put his foot in the way and pushed at the girl with all his might. She fell back into the hallway, jumped up, and ran down the stairs.

"Are you all right?" Jonathan asked as he and Mandie stepped inside the hallway.

"I think so," Mandie replied weakly, but then she crumpled onto the floor.

Jonathan stooped beside her, then quickly stood up and began shouting down the stairs, "Someone get a doctor! Pronto! Doctor! Make haste!"

Mandie protested, "No, no." She tried to stand up and fell down again. The hallway was spinning around. She bent her head, closed her eyes, and tried to breathe deeply.

Jonathan continued yelling for a doctor. Mandie was aware of many people suddenly coming into the hall, and some ventured up the steps to where she sat. In her fuzzy vision, Mandie saw what looked like an elderly, plump woman with jet black hair bend over her and feel her head.

"Sí, sí!" the woman yelled at the others.

Jonathan stooped down beside Mandie and said, "We'll get a doctor. You can't walk all the way back to my house like this."

Mandie shook her head and said, "I don't need a doctor. Besides, the only doctor I know in New York is Dr. Plumbley. Dr. Plumbley."

A buzz went through the crowd that had gathered, and Mandie was faintly aware of a young man rushing down the stairs. The old woman put an arm around Mandie and leaned Mandie's head against her shoulder as she removed Mandie's hat and began stroking her hair.

Mandie could not remember exactly what happened after that, but she suddenly looked up into the worried black face of her dear friend, Dr. Plumbley, and thought she was dreaming.

"My, my, Miss Amanda, what are you all doing here?" Dr. Plumbley asked as he felt for her pulse.

"I knew you'd come," Mandie said through a misty fog. "I wanted to see you anyhow while we are in New York."

"Well, this is a bad way to visit with me," Dr. Plumbley said. "We need to get you back to your friend's house and into bed."

Jonathan tried to explain to the doctor how they had ended up in this tenement building without actually telling him all the details. "We were really lost," he said. "Then we got locked out on the roof. We've been up there for hours."

Dr. Plumbley looked at him and said, "Never mind your explanations. We need to get Miss Amanda back to your house immediately. Do you have transportation?"

"Oh no, we walked over here," Jonathan admitted with a loud sigh.

"Then I have my buggy down on the street. We will take her in it," the doctor decided as he stood up.

Mandie suddenly realized what they were saying and began objecting in a weak voice. "My cat, Snowball. He's somewhere in this building. I have to find him," she protested.

The older woman who had comforted her moved to the top of the stairs and began a loud, rapid string of words that Mandie could not understand. Then suddenly a young girl pushed her way through the crowd on the stairs, and Mandie saw she was carrying Snowball. She stooped to hand him to Mandie.

"Mandie, let me carry Snowball. I'll see that he doesn't get loose again," Jonathan promised as he took the white cat from the girl.

Dr. Plumbley stooped and picked Mandie up in his arms, and the crowd parted to allow him to walk down the stairs.

"Thank you, thank you," Mandie kept mumbling to the people watching as they descended the steps.

The strangers kept jabbering away in their foreign language as Jonathan, holding firmly to the white cat, followed Dr. Plumbley and spoke to the people in their tongue.

Mandie tried to talk on the short ride to Jonathan's house, but she kept running out of breath. She was still not thinking clearly and asked, "Dr. Plumbley, how did you find us?"

"My office is two blocks over from where you were," Dr. Plumbley said. "A Spanish boy came into my office screaming that someone was sick and had asked for me." He looked at her and smiled as she rode securely tucked in between the doctor and Jonathan, who was still holding on to Snowball.

"Thank you, Dr. Plumbley," Mandie said in a cracked voice. "When are you coming to Franklin again?"

"I'd like to come down and visit Abraham sometime after the weather warms up," Dr. Plumbley replied. "I hope your family are all well."

"Yes," Mandie managed to say and then ran out of breath again.

"Mandie came to New York with her friend Celia Hamilton and Celia's mother. My father asked them to stay at our house," Jonathan explained. "Do you know Mandie's family?"

"Why, I sure do," Dr. Plumbley said with a big smile. "I wouldn't be a doctor today if it hadn't been for their generosity. And not only that, they are also helping to educate my nephew who is studying medicine." He looked across the seat at Jonathan and added, "They treat me like kin people."

"I'm not sure how long they are planning to stay, but maybe we could visit before they go home to North Carolina," Jonathan suggested.

Mandie, not exactly coherent with her cold disorienting her, looked up at the doctor and said, "I want you and Moses to come eat Thanksgiving dinner with us."

Dr. Plumbley started to object, but Jonathan quickly said, "Yes, that would be a great idea. We are not having any guests for dinner tomorrow except Mandie and Celia and Mrs. Hamilton. My father had to go to Washington yesterday, but he is supposed to return home this afternoon. I know he would make you both welcome."

"Good idea, Jonathan," Mandie mumbled. "Tell Mrs. Cook two more people are coming." She fell silent and leaned her head on Jonathan's shoulder.

"Please say you and your nephew will come," Jonathan told him, and then with a smile he added, "Besides, we may need you to look at Mandie again tomorrow to be sure she is recuperating from this cold."

"I don't normally go to dinner at other people's

houses unless the man of the house expressly asks me, and you say your father is away," Dr. Plumbley said.

"Which makes me the man of the house right now," Jonathan said proudly. "And it is absolutely all right with my father if I invite people to dinner."

Dr. Plumbley silently looked at Jonathan and then asked, "What time?"

Jonathan grinned and said, "Come early so we can talk. We always have the Thanksgiving dinner at noon, so if you and your nephew could make it a couple hours before that, we'd have time to get acquainted."

"Thank you, young man," Dr. Plumbley said with a nod. "Moses and I will be there about ten o'clock then."

The doctor turned the buggy into the Guyer driveway and pulled up under the portico. Mandie shook her head, trying to clear it, then she saw Jens quickly rush toward the buggy as Jonathan jumped down.

"Jens, the doctor here needs to put Miss Amanda in her bed. She's sick with a cold," Jonathan explained.

"No, no, no," Mandie protested as Dr. Plumbley picked her up out of the buggy. "I don't want to go to bed. Can't I just lie on the settee by the fire?"

"Sure, Mandie," Jonathan said, still holding Snowball, and directed the doctor into the parlor where he deposited Mandie on the settee.

Mrs. Yodkin, evidently hearing the commotion, came rushing in with pillows and quilts. "First, we take off the coat and hat," the housekeeper told Mandie as she sat on the settee and began removing Mandie's outer garments. "And then the shoes come off." She helped Mandie sit back against the pillows and quickly covered her with the quilts. "Now we bring tea, and we bring the cat to the kitchen," the woman added as she took Snowball from Jonathan and left the room.

Dr. Plumbley smiled at Jonathan and said, "You have a very efficient housekeeper, I must say. I was just going to order hot tea and bed rest. Now I have to be going, but we will see you tomorrow. Thank you for the invitation." He shook Jonathan's hand.

Mandie reminded the doctor to be sure he and Moses did come, and the doctor reminded her to behave herself and rest.

Jonathan walked the doctor to the door, then came back into the parlor. He looked around. Everyone but Mandie had vanished. "Where did Jens go? I want to ask him some questions," Jonathan said as he removed his coat and hat and threw them on a nearby chair.

"I will ring for him to come back," Jonathan said. He pulled one of the bell ropes by the window. "He is going to have to answer some questions." He went to stand by the fireplace.

"When Mrs. Yodkin brings the tea for you, I will ask her to tell Jens we want to talk with him in here," Jonathan said.

Mandie started to sit up higher on the settee, then she remembered something. "Jonathan, we'll never find that man again, and we may never see the girl again," she said.

"I expect to get some information from Jens," Jonathan told her.

The butler returned to the parlor and stood in the doorway. "Yes, Master Jonathan," he said.

Mandie waited eagerly to hear the conversation with Jens.

"Jens, Miss Amanda and I have some questions we'd like answered," Jonathan began.

"Yes, Master Jonathan," Jens said politely but with aloofness.

"Miss Amanda saw you giving an envelope to a strange man in the greenery early this morning," Jonathan began. "And then we saw the same man and the girl who tried to claim the dog running out of the house later this morning while you claimed they had tied you up and stolen something. Exactly what is this all about?"

Jens cleared his throat and avoided looking straight into Jonathan's eyes. "I gave the man some money for his Spanish charity, and evidently he thought there was more money in the house and came back to rob us," he explained.

Mandie listened and sensed that the man was not telling everything he knew.

"Who is this man? What is his name?" Jonathan asked.

"I do not know, Master Jonathan. He came begging for his charity," Jens insisted. "And when he returned, he had the girl with him. She kept saying you had stolen her dog."

Mandie raised up a little and asked, "Where is the dog?"

"Oh, he is safe," Jens said. "He has been in the kitchen all morning. Mrs. Yodkin just put him in the back parlor so she can feed the cat in the kitchen. And, I might add, she will be bringing your noonday meal in here since your other guests have not returned."

"Thank goodness we got back before Celia and

her mother did," Mandie whispered hoarsely to Jonathan.

"Jens, I don't believe you are telling me everything you know," Jonathan said to the butler. "Who is that man? You must know or you wouldn't have been so friendly with him. Why did you give him money that you distinctly told him not to tell where he got it? According to Miss Amanda, you also told him not to rush whatever it was he planned to do, because that is not the way we do things. What did you mean by that?"

Jens cleared his throat again and replied, "He wanted to go back to all those Spanish people and tell them where he got the money, and I knew that wouldn't do. They'd all be here begging for more money."

Jonathan looked at Mandie. She thought about that for a moment and then shook her head without Jens seeing her do this, making Jonathan understand that she didn't believe Jens's explanation.

"Where does this man live, Jens? How did you happen to know him?" Jonathan asked.

"But, Master Jonathan, I do not know this man, and I have no idea as to where he lives," Jens denied.

"Yet you gave him an envelope full of money?" Jonathan questioned. "Jens, I don't believe what you are saying."

"I am very sorry, Master Jonathan, but I speak the truth," Jens insisted. "I do make donations to charity now and then, and I believed the man when he said his family did not have any heat or anything to eat."

"When we untied you, you called the man and the girl thieves and said they stole something,"

Jonathan reminded him. "Well, if you don't know what they stole, how do you know they stole anything at all?"

Jens hesitated and then said, "They bragged to me that they had stolen something because you had stolen the girl's dog."

"How did they manage to tie you up? Was there no one else around? Also, how did they get into the house in the first place?" Jonathan asked.

"Master Jonathan, the man knocked on the back door and said he had come to tell me how much his family appreciated the money," Jens replied. "Then before I realized it, he had thrown a rope around me, and the girl was with him. If you remember, all the maids were working upstairs at that time."

"Where was Mrs. Cook? She was supposed to be in the kitchen all morning," Mandie put in. "I left my cat in there, and she said she would watch him. But she wasn't there when we found you, and my cat was running loose."

"I am sorry, miss, but you will have to ask Mrs. Cook," Jens said. "She came into the kitchen right after you two ran out the back door. She said she had seen nothing and did not know those people had tied me up."

"Jens, this is a very puzzling situation, and I believe you could help us clear some of this up if you would tell us the truth," Jonathan said.

Jens tightened his lips and stood up very straight. "I do beg your pardon, Master Jonathan, but I am telling you all the truth that I am aware of."

"How much money did you give the man, Jens?" Jonathan asked.

"Not very much," the butler replied, shifting his

eyes. "Only enough to buy food and heat for his family, and I must say, he has twelve children."

"Twelve children," Mandie exclaimed under her breath. *How could anyone support so many children?*

"Now I will tell you what we know," Jonathan said, still standing by the fireplace while Jens remained just inside the doorway. "Miss Amanda and I followed that man, and he ended up in one of those awful tenement buildings over on the East Side. There must have been dozens and dozens of people living in that one building." He paused and looked at Jens, but the butler did not show any sign of knowledge about this.

"And we also know that girl was there in that building," Jonathan added.

"But, Master Jonathan, you and the miss should not have gone into such a neighborhood. It could have been an ill fate," Jens said.

"As it turned out, we did meet up with problems there," Jonathan said. "We were locked outside on the roof all morning, and that is why Miss Amanda has such a terrible cold."

"I am very sorry, Master Jonathan, but you should have thought twice before you ventured into that cluster of foreigners," Jens said.

"I want you to know that when my father returns, I intend discussing all this matter with him. I am sure he will have more questions for you. You may go about your duties now, Jens," Jonathan said.

"Yes, Master Jonathan," the butler replied and disappeared through the doorway into the hall.

Jonathan shook his head, looked at Mandie, and said, "I just don't know what to make of that conversation with Jens. I'm sure he's not telling the complete truth." He sat down on a chair near the settee where Mandie was lying.

"I don't think he was, either," Mandie agreed.

At that moment Mrs. Yodkin came into the parlor carrying a silver tray with a teapot and china on it. She set it down on a table near Mandie.

"Now I will pour this tea for you, and you must drink every drop," she told Mandie. "We must get you well so you can eat Thanksgiving turkey tomorrow."

Mandie watched as she poured the tea into a cup and handed it to her. "Thank you, Mrs. Yodkin," she said. "I really appreciate your kindness."

Then Monet wheeled in a cart laden with steaming food and parked it near the table. Jonathan stepped over to see what was on it.

"Monet will stay and serve for you," Mrs. Yodkin said as she started to leave the room.

"We can do it, Mrs. Yodkin," Mandie protested.

"Yes, we can wait on ourselves. Thank you, Mrs. Yodkin, Monet," he told the two women.

The two servants looked at each other and then left the room.

"I have to sit up because I think I might be able to eat something. I feel so hungry my stomach hurts," Mandie remarked as she pushed up to a sitting position with her feet and legs still under the quilts. "Everything smells good."

Jonathan grinned as he picked up plates from the cart and said, "That sounds like you're better already."

"I do feel better," Mandie agreed as Jonathan put food on a plate and handed it to her. "But you know, Jonathan, this thing is nowhere settled. We need to find out what that man and that girl were supposed to have stolen, for one thing. And if we could just catch up with that man and talk to him, maybe he would tell us a different story from what Jens did."

"You're right. I was thinking the same thing," Jonathan said, heaping a plate for himself and then sitting near the settee. "I hate to bring my father into this because I'd like to solve everything myself."

"If only we had Uncle Ned here, he would be able to help us. He knows so much about people in general," Mandie remarked as she tasted the potatoes on her plate.

"But this is New York, and Uncle Ned is all the way down in North Carolina, and being Cherokee he just might not have ever been to New York," Jonathan reminded her.

"I think Uncle Ned has been almost everywhere. Remember, he even came to Europe, and he was at President McKinley's second inauguration," Mandie reminded him.

"Do you stay in touch with him? I mean, does he know you have come to New York?" Jonathan asked.

"He always knows where I am," Mandie replied. "When my father died, Uncle Ned promised him he would watch over me, and he always does. My father considered him his best friend. And you know that my father's mother was Cherokee, but Uncle Ned is not actually blood kin."

"I remember you telling me all that," Jonathan replied, hungrily devouring his food.

"I just thought of something," Mandie said, sitting up straighter. "When Celia and her mother come back from shopping, are we going to tell them everything that happened to us today?"

Jonathan thought about that for a moment and said, "We won't if you don't want to."

"I know that her mother will tell my mother about everything we do here in New York, and it would just worry my mother. After all, that terrible ordeal on the roof is over," Mandie explained. "I suppose it would be all right to tell them the rest of the events since they left this morning."

"Then I will speak to my father privately, because I will have to tell him everything," Jonathan said, reaching to refill his plate. "More roast or anything?"

"No, not right now," Mandie said. "In a way, I'll be glad when Celia gets back so we can discuss all this with her. I will tell her everything, but not her mother."

"And she won't tell?" Jonathan questioned.

"No, she's my best friend. We share all our secrets," Mandie replied.

Mandie found herself looking forward to the return of her friend but wondered how she would talk with her right away without her mother present. She would have to think of a way.

Chapter 9 / More Mystery

When Celia and her mother returned from shopping, Mandie and Jonathan were still sitting by the fire in the parlor. Mandie was trying to figure out a way to talk privately with her friend, but the answer came much easier than she had expected.

"How are you feeling, Amanda?" Mrs. Hamilton asked as she looked at Mandie lying under the quilts on the settee.

"I think I'll soon be all right, Mrs. Hamilton," Mandie said with a big smile. She certainly didn't want Celia's mother to worry about her health.

"I hope so. And, Jonathan, did you have a nice day?" Mrs. Hamilton asked. She removed her gloves and began unbuttoning her heavy winter coat.

"It was interesting. But where are your packages? I thought you and Celia went shopping," Jonathan replied, standing by the mantelpiece.

"Everything will be shipped directly to our home

so we don't have to bother with it on our return journey," Mrs. Hamilton said, removing her coat. "Come on now, Celia, and get cleaned up."

Celia had been standing in the middle of the floor looking at the others. Now she smiled at her mother and said, "I'll be right up, Mother. There's something I need to tell Mandie first."

"Well, don't be too long," her mother replied as she left the room.

"What is it, Mandie? You look like the goose that laid the golden egg," Celia said, quickly pulling up a stool by the settee. She took off her gloves and coat and sat down.

"Why, Celia, what on earth are you talking about?" Mandie teased.

"We certainly haven't seen any golden eggs today," Jonathan told her as he sat down in the chair next to them.

"Oh, do tell, Mandie," Celia said, eagerly looking from Jonathan to Mandie. "What have y'all been up to today?"

"Well, you see, it was like this," Mandie began. She quickly related the day's events to her friend with Jonathan adding a comment here and there. Celia's eyes widened as she listened.

"Mandie, how could you even think about going into such a neighborhood?" Celia asked.

"We didn't exactly have time to think. The man was getting away, and we had to follow real fast," Mandie replied.

"Remember, Uncle Ned always tells us to think first and then act?" Celia reminded her. She looked at Jonathan and added, "Jonathan, you must have known that was a dangerous part of town."

"But we didn't see anything dangerous going on

over there," Jonathan told her.

"No, it didn't look dangerous, Celia," Mandie agreed and frowned. "It's just a lot of poor people who don't even know how to speak English."

"And Dr. Plumbley said his office is near there," Jonathan told her.

"And, Celia, he and his nephew Moses are coming here for dinner tomorrow," Mandie said with a big smile. "We asked them, and Jonathan said it would be all right with his father. Mr. Guyer hasn't come home yet."

"You and Jonathan could have been locked out on that roof forever without anyone even knowing where you were. Suppose that girl had not opened the door and it had begun to snow real hard. What would you have done?" Celia asked in disbelief. "And you know these people must be dangerous. After all, you said they tied up the butler and stole something from the house here."

"That's what Jens claims. I plan on asking my father to talk to him," Jonathan said.

"Well, here I am. What is it you want me to talk about, son?" Mr. Guyer asked from the doorway. He walked into the room.

"Oh, Father, I didn't hear you come in," Jonathan said, rising from the chair. "Could we talk privately when you have time?"

"There's no better time than now. Come with me. We'll go up to my study," Mr. Guyer said. He looked at the girls and added, "I hope you young ladies have been enjoying yourselves. Are you feeling under the weather, Miss Amanda, or just resting under those quilts?"

"I'm feeling much better now, thank you, Mr. Guyer," Mandie replied as she sat straight up. "I have a little cold, but I do believe it's about to go away."

"Let's hope so. Now, Jonathan, come on," Mr. Guyer told his son.

"Be back soon," Jonathan told the girls.

"Be sure you tell him everything, and I mean everything, Jonathan," Mandie said in a loud whisper as Mr. Guyer left the room and Jonathan started to follow.

Jonathan gave her a big grin and said as he went out the doorway, "Yes, ma'am, Miss Amanda. That I will do."

Celia stood up and shook out her long skirts as she held her coat and gloves. "Mandie," she said, "I'd better get upstairs before my mother comes looking for me, but I'll be right back."

Mandie looked at her friend and said, "You understand, Celia, that we are not going to tell your mother every little thing we've been doing because she would go and tell my mother, and it would worry her. My mother's still not completely recovered from the fever, you know, and I don't want anything to worry her."

"I am not about to tell my mother all the things you and Jonathan have been saying," Celia promised. "My mother would probably pack up right here and now and take us home. But, Mandie, please try to stay out of danger."

"Oh, go on to your room, Celia," Mandie said with a laugh. "We survived, and I certainly don't plan on doing anything like that again. I learned my lesson."

"I sure hope so," Celia replied, going toward the door to the hallway. "Be right back."

Mandie lay on the settee by herself, reliving the

day's events in her mind, and she was a little fright-
ened when she thought about it. She and Jonathan
could have ended up in a lot of trouble if these people in that tenement house had decided to treat
them as intruders. She silently thanked God for taking care of them.

Sipping the hot tea left in the pitcher on a table
near the settee, she realized she was feeling much
better now. She was glad to have recovered from
the cold and wind on the roof and from the fright of
being up there.

But she wondered who the strange girl and the
foreign-looking man were. She didn't believe what
the butler had told Jonathan about the man. Jens
didn't act just right when he replied to Jonathan's
questions. She wished Jonathan would hurry up
and come back so she could find out what his father
had to say about all this.

Leila, the young maid, interrupted Mandie's
thoughts as she appeared in the doorway to the parlor and asked, "If you are finished with the food cart,
may I take it away?"

Mandie looked at her and smiled as she sat up.
"All done, Leila," she said. "It's all yours."

"Oh, but I do not wish to have it. I only wish to
roll it back to the kitchen if you are finished," Leila
said, smiling back as she walked over and began
stacking some of the dishes on the cart.

"I suppose that means the same thing," Mandie
replied, still smiling. "Where is everyone? Did Jonathan come and talk to all of you?"

"Not Master Jonathan, but Mr. Guyer himself,"
Leila said, looking up from the cart. "Mr. Guyer
himself rang all the bells. All the people in this
house came to the kitchen. He asked questions, but

no one had any answers for him. I did not see the intruders this morning that he asked about, so they sent me for this cart."

"Mr. Guyer is asking questions of all the people who work here," Mandie repeated out loud. Then as Leila began rolling the cart toward the door, she asked, "Is Jens being asked questions, too?"

"Ja, he told us how this man and this girl got in this house this morning and tied him up and stole something, but I know nothing about it. Neither did anyone else," Leila said as she pushed the cart toward the doorway. "I must hurry now." She disappeared into the hallway.

Celia was the next one to come into the parlor. She had changed her clothes and brushed her long, curly auburn hair.

"You look so nice, and I look so terrible. My dress is all crumpled up under these quilts," Mandie said as she fanned the covers to look beneath them. "I will have to go clean up and put on a fresh dress before suppertime."

Celia sat on the low stool again. "I wish you could have gone shopping with us, Mandie," she said. "We were in some stores that had the most beautiful things, and Mother insisted I buy anything I wanted. Now I can't even remember what all I did buy."

"Are you having the stuff shipped to your home, or is yours going to our school?" Mandie asked.

"All of it will go to our house," Celia replied. "Some of it is for Molly—"

"Molly?" Jonathan interrupted as he entered the room and sat down nearby. "Whatever happened to Molly? You're talking about the orphan Mrs. Taft brought back from Ireland when you all returned home back in the summer, aren't you?"

"Right," Celia agreed. "She is still living with us."

"Well, how did she get to your house?" Jonathan asked. "I thought Mandie's grandmother was taking Molly home with her until she could locate the girl's aunt here in the United States."

"When we got home and found Mandie's mother so ill, my mother volunteered to take Molly home with us for the time being, and she's still there," Celia explained. "She's quite a handful, too, still searching for leprechauns and still talking without taking time for a breath." She smiled.

"Jonathan," Mandie asked impatiently, "what did you find out?"

"Absolutely nothing," Jonathan said with a disappointed shrug. "No one saw or heard anyone in the house this morning. And Jens still holds to the story he told me."

"Did your father believe him?" Mandie asked.

Jonathan shook his head and said, "No, but Father told me he had never known Jens to lie about anything before."

"And we don't even know what the man and the girl stole," Mandie said.

"And it would be hard to figure out what is missing in this big house," Celia commented.

"It would be impossible," Jonathan agreed. "My father is thinking about hiring a detective to get information on the man and the girl and to check out the story Jens told us."

"That is a great idea," Mandie said, and then she added, "But in the meantime, we could spy on Jens."

"Spy on Jens?" Celia questioned.

"I'm not sure we could do that without him finding out," Jonathan said. "But we could try. Shall we begin right now?"

"Now?" Mandie asked, tossing back the quilts and swinging her feet to the floor.

"Yes, now," Jonathan replied. "You see, Jens has free time between the noon meal and whenever we eat at night. He only answers the door, or checks on the housekeeper who checks on the maids, so he's free to move around and do anything he likes."

"All right, I'm all for it," Mandie agreed as she stood up. She swallowed and realized her throat was also clearing up. "But I do have to go to my room to change clothes before we eat tonight."

"Father will expect us all down here in the parlor at six o'clock, so we do have some time to spy. Let's go," Jonathan told her.

"Coming, Celia?" Mandie asked, looking at her friend, who had not volunteered to spy with them.

"I suppose so," Celia said as she followed her two friends out of the parlor into the hallway. "Jonathan, where is the dog?" she asked.

"Oh, he's in the back parlor. We'll take him out in the garden later," Jonathan replied. "Now, we should begin somewhere around the kitchen."

The two girls followed Jonathan through several corridors as he cautioned them to be quiet. He softly opened doors along the way, looked inside the rooms, and listened, but there was no sound anywhere until they came to the door of the greenery, which was closed.

Jonathan held up his hand to stop the girls and whispered, "He might be in here. This is a good place for clandestine operations." He grinned.

The three young people peeked through the

glass door, then Jonathan softly pushed it open and led the way inside the glass room, all the time motioning for the girls to be quiet.

Mandie tried to see among the large plants and the huge pots, but she was too short to see over them and the plants were too close together to see through them.

The three silently crept around the room, stooping behind pots and plants. They had gone about halfway across toward the door to the garden when Mandie heard the door open. She put her hand on Celia's arm as Jonathan touched hers. They stayed where they were and waited and listened.

Suddenly there was talking across the room from the three.

"Do not worry, Angelina," a man said. "We will get the white dog for you. Somehow we will do it. Do not worry."

Mandie instantly recognized the voice of the man they had been chasing earlier.

"But how will we do it?" the girl asked.

And Mandie recognized the voice of the girl they had found in the garden. So here the two were, brazen enough to come into Jonathan's house after all that had transpired.

"It's them," Jonathan whispered in Mandie's ear.

Mandie nodded and whispered to Celia, "The man and the girl."

Celia crept closer to Mandie.

Then Mandie heard another sound that she recognized. A loud meow across the room could only come from Snowball. He must have found a way to escape from the kitchen, where he was supposed to be. She sighed to herself and wondered how she would rescue him.

"Your cat," Jonathan whispered in Mandie's ear.

Mandie nodded and whispered back, "Right, and I will have to catch him somehow before he goes outside and disappears."

The man spoke again, "We must go home now, Angelina, and you should not come over here all by yourself any more. You might just disappear. These people are angry with us."

"I want my dog," Angelina insisted. "I want him now."

Snowball meowed loudly again.

"I have idea," the man said. "You hear that white cat? He is here somewhere. We take him. Then people will give us the dog for the cat."

Without thinking, Mandie jumped to her feet and ran across the room, calling to her cat, "Snowball, where are you? Snowball!" She hurried between the rows and rows of greenery.

"Mandie!" Jonathan called to her as he followed.

Celia also got to her feet to assist in the hunt for Snowball.

Mandie came within sight of the man and the girl, who were rushing out the door into the garden. "Wait! We want to talk to you," she called to them.

"Stop!" Jonathan yelled at the strangers.

But the man and the girl disappeared into the tall plants in the garden without even looking back.

"Snowball!" Mandie cried as she finally caught up with the white cat and picked him up. "You just ruined everything!"

Jonathan had gone on out into the garden, and Mandie rushed outside with Celia following her. She saw Jonathan near the gate. From the look on his face she knew the strangers had escaped.

"They got away, and I don't think we'd better go after them. We don't have our coats on, and you are already sick with that cold. Let's go back inside," Jonathan told Mandie.

"It's freezing out here," Celia said as she shivered.

The three hurried back inside the greenery and on into the main part of the huge house. Mandie carried Snowball and wouldn't let him down.

"I'd better check on the dog," Jonathan told the girls as he led the way to the back parlor.

When he opened the door, the white dog was lying on the hearth beside a brightly lit fireplace. The animal saw Jonathan and quickly rose and came to greet him. He wanted to jump up and down all over Jonathan, but Jonathan told him, "Now, now, down, boy. You are not allowed to do that, remember?" He stooped to rub the dog's head.

The dog obeyed immediately and stood there enjoying the petting.

"He does belong to someone," Jonathan said, looking up at the girls. "I just wish I knew how to find the owner. Even though I'd like to keep him myself, whoever he belongs to may be out searching the streets for him."

"And you don't think he really belongs to that girl? What's her name? Angelina?" Celia asked.

"Never," Jonathan said emphatically. "He doesn't want anything to do with her. You saw how he acted when she tried to coax him away before."

"And the man thought he was going to steal Snowball," Mandie said as she hugged the cat tightly in her arms.

"He'd sure be sorry," Celia commented.

Jonathan stood up and said, "I think I'd better get my coat and hat and take the dog outside for a little while. Are you girls coming with me?"

"No, I'd better go up to my room and change clothes. I'm a mess," Mandie said, looking down at her dress, soiled from the adventure on the roof. "Why, Jonathan, I do believe you have already changed yours."

"Yes, while I was talking to my father I did a quick job at trying to look more presentable. After all, we did get in a mess on the dirty roof," Jonathan said with a big grin.

"No more roofs for me," Mandie said with a smile. "We haven't even seen Jens yet, and that is what we were doing in the first place, looking for him, when we came to the glass room."

"That's all right. He lives here. We'll spy on him later," Jonathan promised. "Let's meet back in the front parlor in a little while."

The girls agreed, and Celia went with Mandie to their bedroom. When they got in the room, Mandie noticed the door to the adjoining room was open. Evidently, Mrs. Hamilton had already gone downstairs.

"We at least got some information," Mandie commented, setting the cat down and going to the wardrobe to take down a clean dress.

"Some information?" Celia questioned as she flopped into a big chair.

"Yes, we now know the strange girl's name is Angelina," Mandie said with a big smile. "Pretty name for such a wild girl." She went toward the bathroom.

"And the man does speak and understand English," Celia commented. "You said he was speaking a foreign language to Jens when you overheard them before."

"He was," Mandie said as she stopped to look at Celia. Then she added, "I can't imagine why, because Jens was speaking English to him."

"Do you think they sneaked into the house, trying to steal the dog?" Celia asked.

"Probably," Mandie said. "And come to think of it, the gate was open, so they must have just come into the garden through the gate."

"But wouldn't you think the gate would be open sometimes? After all, delivery people have to get in—the milkman, the grocer, the gardener, or whoever."

"I suppose so, but if you remember, Jonathan locked the gate and put the key in his pocket when we were in there before. He got the key from somewhere around the back porch, but he didn't put it back."

"I remember," Celia agreed.

"I'll have to think and ask Jonathan about that," Mandie said as she continued into the bathroom. "I'll hurry so we can get back downstairs."

Mandie was eager to inquire about the garden gate key.

Chapter 10 / A New York Night

When Mandie and Celia returned to the parlor, Jonathan was already there with his father and Celia's mother.

"I was just coming up to see you girls," Jane Hamilton began as the two entered the room. "Jonathan's father has suggested that we all dine out tonight."

The three young people quickly exchanged glances. Mandie, who was never a hearty eater anyway, answered, "If you don't mind, Mrs. Hamilton, I think I'd like to stay here. I'm not really very hungry, and I still feel all worn out."

"Yes, of course, dear. That cold has dampened your spirits," Mrs. Hamilton told her. She looked at Jonathan and Celia.

"Why don't I stay here and keep Mandie company? We can get Mrs. Cook to fix us something when we get hungry," Jonathan replied as he looked at Mandie.

"Then I'll just stay here, too," Celia said. "We did have a busy day today with all that shopping."

Mandie silently breathed a sigh of relief. She understood that her friends were more interested in what was going on in this house than eating out in a fancy restaurant. They would get a chance to spy on Jens.

"Then you and I, Jane, will do up the town tonight," Mr. Guyer said with a big smile as he looked at Mrs. Hamilton across the room.

Mrs. Hamilton looked at the young people and asked, "Are y'all sure you'll be all right here alone?"

Jonathan laughed and said, "I am alone lots of times with the servants while my father travels. We'll be all right. Please don't worry about us."

Mrs. Hamilton looked at Mr. Guyer, and he said, "That is true. I am gone quite a bit, but with all the servants we have living here, they'll be safe. Now I will telephone the restaurant and reserve a table." He stood up.

"And I need to get dressed," Mrs. Hamilton said as she rose.

The two left the room, and the three young people hovered together on the settee.

"Thank goodness we didn't tell her everything that happened today," Jonathan said with a sigh of relief. "But of course my father knows, and he didn't seem worried about it."

Mandie anxiously leaned forward and asked, "Jonathan, the gate in the garden was open when that man and the girl ran away from us. You had the key when we were in there before, and you put it in your pocket. How did the gate get unlocked?"

"Oh, that's easy," Jonathan said with a big grin.

"There must be half a dozen keys to that gate. They're kept in different places because so many people need to go in and out during the day. The gate might have been left open by the servants for a deliveryman to come in, or whatever."

"If that man and this girl, Angelina, live in that tenement house we were in, they have quite a distance to go to get here, but they seem to keep turning up," Mandie said.

"Maybe they don't go all the way home in between the times they come here," Jonathan said.

"I can't imagine why they keep coming back when they know they will most likely be seen," Celia remarked.

"I believe the girl is trying to take the dog," Jonathan said. "She is so insistent that he belongs to her."

"Well, she had better not steal Snowball," Mandie said emphatically. "I left him shut up in our room. Everytime I leave him in the kitchen he gets out."

"You can bring him down here later and I'll get him something to eat," Jonathan told her. "My father will tell Mrs. Cook that he and Mrs. Hamilton are going out to eat, and I can ask her to serve our food in here if you girls want to do that."

"I have a better idea," Mandie said, smiling. "Why don't we just go to the kitchen and eat, and that way I can watch Snowball. He might get food on something in here."

"That's Mrs. Cook's territory, and she might not like us eating there," Jonathan replied.

"Oh, then I have another idea," Mandie replied quickly. "I remember seeing some small tables and chairs in one corner of the glass room. If we ate in there, we could keep a lookout for that girl and that man to return. What do you say?''

"But, Mandie, they would see us and not even come in," Celia reminded her.

"We could move one of the tables behind some of those tall plants," Jonathan suggested.

"And think about how many times we've seen those people in that room," Mandie reminded her friends.

"I believe they go in there because that outside door is never locked," Jonathan explained. "Of course, the doors from the greenery into the rest of the house are locked at night, and they couldn't get into the house from there."

"What will the servants think if we eat in there?" Celia asked.

Jonathan looked at her and grinned as he said, "We won't tell them. We'll just ask for the food to be brought in here, and as soon as they leave the room we'll take it all out there. Besides, we don't want anyone to know we're planning to sit our there. Remember, we're supposed to be spying on Jens."

"Right," Mandie agreed.

"You will have to secure Snowball somehow out there, or he'll run around the room," Celia cautioned her.

"You can be sure I'll tie him up," Mandie said. "I don't want that girl to have a chance to steal him."

As soon as Mr. Guyer and Mrs. Hamilton came back to the parlor and then left for the restaurant, the three young people began implementing their plans.

First they went to the greenery and moved a small table and three chairs into a secluded corner of the room. Then Jonathan went to the kitchen to tell Mrs. Cook they would be eating in the parlor. Mandie hurried up to her room and got Snowball.

Later when Leila brought the food on the cart to the parlor, Jonathan told her, "Thank you, Leila. We'll serve ourselves. I'll ring when we're finished."

"Yes, Master Jonathan," the young girl said with a smile as she left the room.

"Now, I know a shortcut," Jonathan told Mandie and Celia as he stood up and took hold of the handles of the cart. "Just follow me and keep an eye out for servants."

The girls followed him through a back corridor. Luckily the cart was noiseless on the carpeted floors. Mandie carried Snowball in her arms. When they arrived at the door to the greenery, she and Celia held the door open for Jonathan to roll the cart through. But once they were inside the glass room, they found the cart would not fit through the narrow walkway to where they had set up the table and chairs in the dim lighting used for the plants.

"We'll just have to leave the cart here and carry our food to the table, I suppose," Jonathan told the girls, looking around the room.

"That's all right. It's just a few steps behind these plants to the table," Mandie said. "I'll tie Snowball's leash to the table leg so he can't run away. He's used to that when we travel, so he shouldn't make a fuss about it."

Celia and Jonathan began uncovering the dishes on the cart while Mandie secured Snowball.

"Just the aroma of all this food makes me ravenous," Jonathan exclaimed as he looked to see what was in the dishes.

"Me too," Celia agreed.

Mandie came rushing back to the cart and said,

"I hope no one comes in here and starts looking for the source of that smell."

"Yes, we'd better hurry and eat," Jonathan said. "Help yourselves, girls."

The three loaded their plates and took them to the table where they quickly devoured the food. They carried on their conversation in whispers for fear of someone coming in and discovering them. Snowball hungrily cleaned off his plate under the table and then curled up near Mandie's feet. Once they were finished eating, they quietly returned their dishes to the cart.

"Do you think we should take the cart back to the parlor?" Celia asked.

"You hold the door for me and I'll take it back," Jonathan whispered back.

Mandie watched Snowball while Celia helped Jonathan with the cart.

"Be right back," Jonathan told them as he went down the corridor with the food cart.

As soon as Celia sat down next to Mandie at the table, Snowball began squirming around and meowing.

"Oh no," Mandie said with a big sigh. "He wants his sandbox."

"I'll stay here while you take him upstairs," Celia offered.

Mandie bent down and picked up the white cat. "That'll take too long," she said, looking around the room. "Don't you think it would be all right if I just set him in one of these big pots full of dirt?" She glanced at Celia.

"I'm not sure, Mandie," Celia replied as she rose from her chair.

Snowball squirmed vigorously in her arms, and

Mandie said, "I don't think I have time to consider it." She rushed to the nearest huge pot that didn't have anything growing in its dirt and set Snowball inside it.

And at that moment the outside door to the greenery faintly squeaked as it was opened.

Mandie caught her breath and held tightly to the end of Snowball's leash. Celia cautiously crept to her side. The two stood there waiting and trying to see through the maze of plants and pots. There was only silence.

Mandie was beginning to think she had imagined the squeak when suddenly there was a sound behind them. She whirled around to see Jonathan hurrying toward them. And at the same time there was the sound of running feet on the other side of the room.

"Jonathan, quick. That end of the room," Mandie called to him, pointing ahead.

Jonathan instantly turned in that direction and disappeared between the plants. Mandie picked up Snowball and ran the other way, holding the cat in her arms. Celia started down the center of the room.

And it was Celia who suddenly screamed, "Here!" which was followed by the sound of a struggle.

Mandie and Jonathan rushed that way and found Celia struggling to hold Angelina by her long dark hair as the two of them kicked and fought. Mandie grabbed one of the girl's arms and Jonathan got the other one.

"What are you doing in my house again?" Jonathan demanded as the girl sat down on the floor and looked up at him. "Get up!"

Celia reached down to grasp Angelina's hair

again, and the girl immediately stood up. "Don't pull my hair!" she said, trying to slap at Celia, but Mandie and Jonathan managed to grab her hands.

"I asked you a question. What are you doing in my house?" Jonathan repeated in a stern voice.

"I want my dog," the girl said, looking from him to the girls.

"That white dog does not belong to you, and you might as well stop saying he does because no one believes you," Jonathan told her. "And this is my house, not yours."

The girl frowned and did not answer.

"We know your name is Angelina," Mandie said. "What is your last name? Angelina what?"

"None of your business," Angelina said, trying to kick at Mandie.

"We are not going to let you go until you answer our questions, so you might as well begin talking," Jonathan ordered.

"My name is Angelina Phipps, so let me go now," the girl said.

"Phipps?" Jonathan questioned her. "Did you say Phipps?"

"Angelina Phipps is who I am," she replied.

"Jens's last name is Phipps. Are you related to him?" Jonathan asked.

"No, I am not, that mean old man," the girl said sharply.

"Who is the man that comes here with you? Is he your father?" Mandie asked her.

The girl looked at her and said, "He is my uncle Mario. I do not have a father."

"Where is your mother then?" Mandie asked.

The girl's face grew sad as she said slowly, "She died."

"Oh, I'm sorry, Angelina," Celia told her.

"But this uncle of yours, Mario, knows our butler, Jens, doesn't he?" Jonathan asked, watching her closely.

"They lived in the same place back in Spain," she replied.

"Spain? Why, Jens is from England," Jonathan said.

"I know nothing else. Now I am going home," she said and somehow managed to suddenly free her hands.

"If I catch you back on our property again I will call the police to you. Do you understand that, Angelina?" Jonathan asked as the girl edged her way toward the outside door. "Go on home and never, ever come back here."

As the girl disappeared through the outside door, the three young people looked at each other and started walking back toward the door into the house. As soon as they stepped inside the corridor, Jonathan reached back and turned the latch on the door.

"It didn't do us much good to catch her, did it?" Celia said as they made their way back to the parlor.

"She said her name is Phipps. She may just be a relative of Jens's," Jonathan said thoughtfully as they went inside the parlor and sat down by the fireplace.

Mandie glanced around the room and said, "The food cart is already gone."

Celia and Jonathan both scanned the parlor.

"I suppose someone took it away as soon as I left it," Jonathan said.

"I wonder if anyone missed us and the cart while we had it out in the glass room?" Mandie said.

"One of the servants could have come in here to see if everything was all right while we were gone," Jonathan reasoned. "I sure hope it wasn't Jens."

"Because if it was Jens, he might have figured we were in the glass room?" Mandie questioned.

"Exactly," Jonathan said. "However, if he came to the greenery, I sure didn't hear or see him."

"Too late to worry about it now," Celia said.

"It doesn't matter. Whoever got it knows that I ramble all around the house all the time, and they probably thought we had gone to the game room or the back parlor," Jonathan said. Then he stood up and added, "The dog. I almost forgot about the poor dog. I'm not sure anyone has fed him. He's supposed to still be in the back parlor. I'd better go see."

"I'll go with you," Mandie said, rising and picking up Snowball.

"And I will, too," Celia added as she stood up and followed them into the hallway.

When Jonathan opened the door to the back parlor, he found the room empty. "He's not here," he said in alarm. "I'd better ask Mrs. Cook if she knows where he is."

The girls followed Jonathan to the kitchen where Mrs. Cook was finishing her duties for the day. She turned from the sink to look at them.

"That dog, Master Jonathan, if I may say so, he needs a little looking after once in a while," the woman said. "Shut up all day in that parlor—he needs fresh air and exercise. That's no way to treat a dog, 'tis not."

"I'm sorry, Mrs. Cook. I've never had a dog before, and I don't know how to take care of one too well. But where is the dog?" Jonathan asked anxiously, looking around the room.

"With Leila. I tell Leila to take him out in the garden, then I will feed him," Mrs. Cook said, turning back to the dishes in the sink.

"In the garden with Leila? Thank you, Mrs. Cook," Jonathan said, quickly turning and leaving the room.

The girls followed him to the back door where he stepped outside to look for Leila and the dog.

"I'll stay right here, Jonathan. It's too cold to go outside," Mandie told him as she stopped in the doorway.

"It's freezing," Celia added, standing beside Mandie.

The girls watched as Jonathan ran across the garden calling for the dog. "Here, boy, here. Where are you?"

Finally they heard Leila answer. "Here he is, Master Jonathan."

Mandie could hear the dog's happy yelps as he evidently saw Jonathan.

When Jonathan came within sight, holding the dog's leash with Leila following, Mandie heard the maid say, "Master Jonathan, there was a girl come into the garden wanting to take the dog. I tell her she cannot, and she tried to pull his leash, but the dog he did not like that and he barked at her. Then she ran away."

Jonathan stopped and looked at the young maid. "Thank you for telling me, Leila," he said. "No one is to ever take this dog unless I tell you myself."

"Ja, Master Jonathan. I understand," Leila replied as they reached the doorway.

"I will take him to the kitchen to feed him. Thank you," Jonathan told the girl, who went down the hallway.

"Angelina must have seen Leila with the dog after we let her go from the greenery," Jonathan remarked as they went back to the kitchen.

"Luckily she wasn't able to take him," Mandie said.

In the kitchen Mrs. Cook set a bowl of food down by the cookstove, and the dog greedily ate every bite as the three young people watched.

"I'll take him up to the front parlor with us, and then I'll keep him in my room tonight, Mrs. Cook. Thank you," Jonathan told the woman as they left the kitchen.

"Be sure you do," Mrs. Cook called after him.

When they got back to the parlor, the dog stretched out on the hearth in the warmth of the fire and went to sleep while Mandie, Celia, and Jonathan discussed the happenings of the evening. Snowball hissed at the dog once and then settled down near him.

"We haven't seen Jens all evening," Jonathan remarked.

"Is he usually around this time of day?" Mandie asked.

"Most of the time," Jonathan said.

"Maybe he went out somewhere," Celia suggested.

"Did he take your father and Celia's mother to the restaurant in the motorcar?" Mandie asked.

Jonathan glanced at her and said, "I would think my father would take the carriage tonight because of the possibility of snow. The motorcar is too open and too hard to handle in bad weather."

"Then it would be Hodson driving the carriage and not Jens?" Mandie asked.

"I'm not sure. Most of the time it is, but I think I'll go check," Jonathan said as he stood up. "If you girls would watch the dog for me, I'll be right back."

He was gone only a few minutes. And he looked puzzled as he entered the parlor.

"Well?" Mandie asked.

"Hodson did drive Father and Mrs. Hamilton in the carriage, but Mrs. Yodkin says immediately after they left, Jens came and told her he was going on an errand and would be back shortly. He has not returned yet," Jonathan explained as he sat down.

"Maybe it turned out to be a longer errand than he expected," Celia said.

"I've never known him to go out like that when Hodson was gone. It has always been the rule that one of them is here at all times," Jonathan stated.

"More mystery all the time," Mandie said with a loud sigh. "I suppose we will just have to sit here and wait for him to come back, and then you can ask him where he's been."

Jonathan grinned at her and said, "I'll leave that up to my father, thank you."

"I understand," Mandie said, giving him a big smile. "We can't solve all the mysteries around this big house."

She had no idea how long Celia's mother and Jonathan's father would be out, but she imagined the three of them would be asleep long before that. This was New York, and things weren't normal to her here.

Chapter 11 / Whose Dog Is It Anyhow?

Tired out by the day's activities and the cold, Mandie decided to go to bed about eleven o'clock. And Celia, after walking what she called miles that day shopping, readily agreed that she, too, would like to retire.

"Jonathan, are you going to check on Jens again?" Mandie asked as they rose from their seats near the fireplace in the parlor. She picked up her white cat.

"Yes, one more time. You girls just wait here for a minute, and I'll see whether he has returned or not," Jonathan told them as he left the parlor.

The white dog rose from the hearth, stretched, and yawned.

"Now you just stay put," Mandie told the animal. "Jonathan will be back in a minute."

The dog looked up at her as though he understood. Snowball stiffened in her arms and growled at him.

Celia stooped down to pat the dog on the head. To her surprise the dog sat down and closed his eyes, evidently enjoying the attention. "It's a shame that someone has lost such an intelligent dog."

But the minute Jonathan came back into the parlor, the dog jumped up and ran to him.

"Jens is not back yet," Jonathan said as he reached for the dog's leash on a table nearby and hooked it on his collar. "I'm going to take the dog out into the garden for a minute, and then I am going to bed, too. I'll let him sleep by my bed."

"Do you suppose Jens will come back home tonight?" Mandie asked.

"If he wants his job, he had better. I imagine he is already in pretty deep trouble by even going out tonight," Jonathan replied as he stood up and held the end of the dog's leash.

"Good night," Mandie said. "We'll see you bright and early in the morning."

"Good night," Jonathan replied as they left the parlor.

"Be sure you close your bedroom door so the dog can't get out," Celia reminded him as they went to their different rooms.

Once in their room, the girls discussed the happenings of the day. After they had dressed for bed and crawled beneath the covers, they were both soon asleep.

Sometime later Mandie was awakened by Snowball's loud growling on her bed. She reached for him but he moved down the counterpane.

"Snowball, what is wrong with you?" she asked

sleepily, pulling the covers up around her shoulders.

Snowball leaped off the bed and landed with a thud on the carpet as he continued to growl. Mandie sat up to see what he was doing. She fumbled with the switch on the electric lamp by the bed and blinked when the bright light came on. The cat was crouched by the bottom of the door to the hall and still growling.

"What is it?" Celia asked in a whisper as she, too, sat up.

"There is something or some person outside that door," Mandie replied, swinging her legs over the side of the high bed and sliding to her feet.

"Mandie, you are not going to open the door, are you?" Celia asked in fright. She huddled under the covers as she watched.

"How are we going to know what's out there if I don't open the door?" Mandie whispered back. She slowly crept toward the door.

Just as Mandie put her hand on the doorknob to open it, Snowball suddenly hushed and jumped back onto the bed and began washing his face. She slowly opened the door far enough to peep out. There was no one in sight. The light was burning in the lamp at the far end of the hallway and there was no noise.

"Well, I don't know what's going on," Mandie said to herself as she started to close the door. Then a glimpse of movement at the intersection of the corridor with the cross hall caught her eye. She frowned, trying to see better.

"Mandie, please close that door," Celia whispered from the bed.

Suddenly Mandie made out the figure lurking in

the shadows. She quickly reached behind the door to grab her robe from the chair where she had left it, and as she hastily put it on she called to Celia, "Come on. It's that girl, Angelina."

Mandie raced out the door and down the hallway. Looking back she saw Celia following, putting on her robe as she ran. But by glancing back she lost sight of Angelina, and when she came to the intersection of the two corridors, she couldn't decide which way to go.

"She's disappeared," Mandie whispered to Celia who had caught up with her. "You go that way and I'll go this way. Holler if you see her." Mandie went to the right and motioned Celia to the left.

Celia hesitated a moment and then went running down the other hallway. Mandie was careful to look behind the various pieces of furniture that were sitting along the wide corridor, but the only thing she found was Snowball who had somehow got ahead of her. She snatched him up and held him tightly in her arms.

After turning more corners, Mandie and Celia eventually caught up with each other and stopped to catch their breath.

"She got away," Mandie said with a disappointed sigh.

Suddenly the white dog came running toward them. Angelina was in hot pursuit. Evidently she didn't see the two girls, who immediately ducked behind a settee sitting in an alcove in the hallway.

"Let's stop her," Mandie whispered to Celia as she held on to Snowball. "When she gets even with that door over there, we'll grab her."

Celia didn't have time to agree because the girl came near them and was so intent on capturing the dog she didn't see Mandie. Letting go of Snowball, Mandie leaped out and grabbed the girl's skirt.

"Stop that!" Angelina cried out loudly as Mandie pulled her to the floor and Celia helped hold her there.

"What are you doing in this house again?" Mandie demanded, holding tightly to the girl's arm.

The white dog had stopped and came toward them, loudly barking.

"My dog!" the girl insisted as she tried to break loose from Mandie's hands.

"What's going on?" Jonathan called to them as he came running down the hallway. Seeing Angelina, he didn't wait for an answer but added, "Well now, I suppose I will have to call the police just like I told you I would if you came back into this house again." He stooped to look at her as Mandie and Celia held her on the floor.

"Jonathan, how did the dog get out of your room?" Mandie asked.

"I don't know," he answered in puzzlement, looking at the white dog that was happily licking his lips and watching the commotion. "I do know I closed the door because Celia reminded me to do that."

"My dog!" Angelina insisted as she tried to get up.

"Did you open my door and let the dog out?" Jonathan asked.

"That's my dog, not yours!" the girl told him angrily.

"So we know how the dog got out of my room," Jonathan said, looking at Mandie and Celia.

Suddenly there was a voice down the hallway "Angelina, where are you?" As the person go closer and turned the corner toward them, the three young people saw Jens hurrying in their direction. At the same time he saw them and rushed forward to say, "Master Jonathan, I see you have caught up with Angelina. I tried to put her out of the house but lost her in the hallways."

Jonathan stood up and looked at the butler. He was dressed in his usual uniform. "And how did you know Angelina was in the house?" Jonathan asked.

"Why, I saw her fleeing down the hallway," Jens replied. "Do you wish me to remove her now?"

"Of course, Jens. You know she should not be in this house," Jonathan told the man. "I want you to see that she is put outside and all the windows and doors are locked so she cannot get back in. And if you do see her again, I want you to call the police. Is this understood?"

"Yes, Master Jonathan," Jens replied, bending down to grasp one of Angelina's hands and pull her to her feet.

Mandie and Celia released the girl and stood up.

Jonathan leaned over to look closer at the pocket of Angelina's coat, and he suddenly snatched a handkerchief hanging half out. Angelina tried to grab it, but Jonathan moved out of reach. As he unfolded the lace-trimmed square of white material, a small metal tag fell into his hands.

"Is this what you stole from this house?" Jonathan asked, holding up the handkerchief and flipping over the metal tag to read the inscription.

"I did not steal it. Jens said I could have it," Angelina insisted.

Jonathan looked at Jens and asked, "Is this what you were talking about when you said this girl and that man stole something?"

"I believe so, Master Jonathan. Now I shall get rid of this urchin," Jens said and began walking down the corridor, practically dragging the girl with him.

Jonathan didn't say anything else but stood there smoothing out the handkerchief.

Mandie moved closer and looked at it. "Why, that's my handkerchief!" she exclaimed. "See my name on it? Amanda. She must have taken that from my room. Only, I am not sure I brought any of those handkerchiefs with me."

Jonathan looked at her and grinned as he said, "You certainly didn't bring this one with you. Don't you remember where this came from?"

Celia quickly said, "From the ship, Mandie."

Mandie became flustered and said, "From the ship. When I waved good-bye to you and your father from the ship we sailed on from England last summer, I accidentally dropped my handkerchief."

"And I caught it," Jonathan added with a slight blush.

"You mean you kept it all this time?" Mandie stammered as she couldn't think of anything else to say.

"Of course. I wouldn't throw away such a dainty thing as this," he said, still grinning.

"I think I'd better go back to bed," Celia said, turning to walk back down the hallway.

"I'm coming," Mandie said, quickly snatching up Snowball.

"Wait. This tag may belong to the dog," Jonathan said, stopping the girls. He held it out. "See what it says. On one side, 'My name is Whitey,' and on the other side is the name Titus with an address."

Mandie took it, and Celia turned back to join her in reading it.

Mandie looked at Jonathan and said, "Angelina probably removed this tag from the dog's collar. What are you going to do about it?"

Jonathan shifted his feet and didn't look at her as he replied, "I suppose I'll have to go to that address and ask if they have a dog missing."

"Oh, Jonathan, and you wanted to keep the dog so badly," Celia said.

"I do, but the right thing to do would be to return him to his owner if I can find whoever that is," Jonathan said as Mandie handed the tag back to him. "I'll speak to my father about it in the morning."

"We'd better all get some sleep. It must be almost morning now," Celia reminded them.

"If you look up that address on the tag, I'd like to go with you, Jonathan," Mandie told him.

Jonathan grinned and said, "We might have to walk some more elevated railroad tracks."

"Oh, good night, Jonathan," Mandie said, laughing as she and Celia walked toward their room and Jonathan and the dog went in the opposite direction.

Mandie and Celia went straight to bed, but when Mandie opened her sleepy eyes in the morning, she felt like the night had been awfully short. She lay there a few minutes thinking about the events that had taken place in the wee hours.

"Good morning, Mandie," Celia called to her from her bed.

"Good morning, Celia," Mandie replied, propping up on the pillows. "I wonder if your mother had already come back and gone to bed when all that happened last night."

"No, Mandie, she had not. I looked in her room when I went in the bathroom after we came back to our room," Celia replied. "And I looked at the clock. It was only five minutes to midnight, so we had not been asleep very long."

Mandie jumped out of bed and went to sit on the carpet in front of the fireplace. Someone had made a fire even though the room was warm with heat from the furnace. Snowball followed her and curled up in the warmth.

"Don't you think we ought to get dressed and see if Jonathan is up?" Celia asked as she slid off her bed. "We don't want to be late for breakfast."

"Right," Mandie agreed, going to the wardrobe to take down a dress. "And I want to go with Jonathan to that address on the dog's tag."

"My mother will have to give us permission, so I hope she comes to breakfast on time," Celia remarked as the two began getting dressed.

And when they got to the parlor downstairs, the girls were surprised to see that Mr. Guyer, Mrs. Hamilton, and Jonathan were all there and waiting for them.

"Father says I may go check out this address provided Hodson takes me in the carriage, and Mrs. Hamilton has agreed for you girls to go along if you wish," Jonathan told them as they came into the room.

"Oh, thank you, Mrs. Hamilton," Mandie said.

"I appreciate your letting me go, Mother," Celia told her.

Mr. Guyer looked at the girls and said, "You will have to hurry through breakfast, get over there, and hurry back. Just in case you all have forgotten, today is Thanksgiving, and Miss Amanda, your doctor friend and his nephew are coming to eat with us."

"Oh, that's right," Mandie said. "Jonathan, is that address close enough for us to get over there and back before Dr. Plumbley and Moses arrive? Remember, he said they would be here about ten o'clock."

"Oh, sure, with Hodson driving us it won't take very long," Jonathan told her. "Now that we're all here, let's eat."

As soon as they finished breakfast, the three young people climbed into the carriage that Hodson had waiting and drove to the address on the dog tag.

Mandie looked out the window as the vehicle came into a clean middle class neighborhood of brownstone houses and stopped in front of one with lace curtains in the windows.

"Here it is," Jonathan told the girls as Hodson opened the carriage door and the three stepped down from the carriage.

"I hope the people are home," Mandie said as she and Celia followed Jonathan up the front steps.

Jonathan looked at the house number on the single front door and said, "Must be just one family living here." He rang the bell in the door.

Almost immediately the door opened. A middle-aged man stood there looking at them. He was tall and slim, his dark hair was slightly gray, and he smiled at them. "May I help you?" he asked.

"Sir, I am Jonathan Guyer, and I live just a few blocks over that way," Jonathan said, waving his hand back in the direction from which they had come. "I wanted to inquire . . . ah . . . do you have—have you lost a—ah, dog lately, sir?"

The man frowned slightly and said, "Yes, as a

matter of fact, I have. But that's nothing unusual. You see, I live alone and I work long hours. The dog gets lonely and manages to break out of his pen in the backyard and run away. He comes back after a while. Why do you ask?"

"Are you Mister Titus?" Jonathan asked.

"That's my name, Jonathan Titus. You see, we have the same first name," the man said with a smile.

"Yes, sir," Jonathan agreed. "Would you please tell me what your dog looks like?"

"He's white, a mixed breed, but very intelligent, I must say, and he's about two years old, I believe," Mr. Titus told him. "And, oh, he wears a tag on his collar with his name on it. I call him Whitey. Have you seen him?"

Jonathan opened his fist and held out the tag on the palm of his hand. "Is this his tag, sir?"

The man took the tag and turned it over, looking alarmed. "Where did you get this? Did something happen to Whitey?"

"Oh no, sir, that is, nothing bad. You see, he turned up in our garden a few days ago, and we just found the tag last night. But if he's your dog, we'll bring him home," Jonathan said with a sad look on his face.

"Oh, Jonathan, you won't be able to keep him after all," Mandie said.

"We'll help you find another dog, Jonathan, one that you can buy and keep," Celia added.

The man looked at the three young people and then asked, "Did you want to keep him, Jonathan?"

Jonathan smiled and said, "He and I have become pretty good friends, and I've never had a dog before."

"Would your family allow you to keep a dog?" Mr. Titus asked.

"Oh, sure, my father has already said I could keep the dog, that is, until we found this tag and knew he must belong to you," Jonathan replied.

"Come in and sit down a few minutes. Let's talk this thing over," Mr. Titus told Jonathan, stepping back and pushing the door wide open.

Mandie looked around as they went through a large foyer and entered a parlor. The man might live alone, but he certainly did have a nice, neat house.

After sitting and talking for a few minutes, Mr. Titus said, "You know, I've been thinking I should find a home for Whitey. I am gone such long hours, and he is alone back there in his pen. I've thought that if I could find the right place, he would be much better off. He has been lonely ever since my wife died last year. Now, I tell you what. Why don't you go home and talk this over with your father, then ask him to ring me on the telephone and we'll see what we can do about Whitey?"

Jonathan stood up instantly and exclaimed, "Oh, thank you, Mr. Titus!" But then he frowned and added, "But I couldn't take your dog. You would miss him, too."

"No, no, that's no problem. As I said, I see very little of him. Now go on home and ask your father to talk to me," Mr. Titus said, rising from his chair and going to a small desk nearby. "Here, I'll write down the number for him to call." He handed Jonathan a slip of paper. "You must hurry now, because I may have to go to work. Since today is Thanksgiving, a day for families to get together, I volunteered to fill in if they need me, although this is my day off.''

"What kind of work do you do, Mr. Titus?'' Mandie asked as they all walked toward the front door.

"I'm a policeman, miss, and most of the men are married with families. I don't mind rescheduling my time so they can be with their families today,'' Mr. Titus said. "Now make haste, Jonathan.''

Mr. Titus waved to them as they entered the carriage and Hodson drove off.

Jonathan was so full of joy he could hardly sit still the short distance back to his house. "This is wonderful, actually owning Whitey,'' he said.

"I'm glad for you, Jonathan,'' Mandie said. "But remember, a pet takes a lot of time and trouble. I know. Snowball keeps me busy.''

"But it's worth it all,'' Jonathan said. "Whitey and I have already become pretty good friends. Oh, I can't believe it.''

When they arrived back at Jonathan's house, the three young people rushed to the parlor where they found Mr. Guyer and Mrs. Hamilton. Jonathan gave his father the slip of paper with Mr. Titus's phone number on it, and his father immediately went to the telephone to call the man. It was all settled in a matter of minutes.

Mandie removed her hat and coat and said, "I'd better get upstairs and hang these up before Dr. Plumbley and Moses arrive.'' She started toward the hallway.

"Amanda,'' Mrs. Hamilton called to her. "Wait just a minute. You don't have to rush because Dr. Plumbley rang up on the telephone a few minutes ago to say he and his nephew won't be able to come. It seems there has been an accident. Several people have been injured in an old building that just collapsed.''

"Oh no!" Mandie replied.

"Where is the building, Mrs. Hamilton?" Jonathan asked, glancing at Mandie.

Mrs. Hamilton looked at Mr. Guyer.

"I believe it's one of those tenements over on the East Side," Mr. Guyer explained.

"Do you know the street?" Jonathan asked as the girls listened.

"No, but Jens seemed to know. Why? Do you know someone over there?" his father asked.

"Later, Father," Jonathan said and quickly left the room.

"Well, I'll go hang up my coat and hat in my room," Mandie said as she started for the door.

"I will, too," Celia added as she followed.

Mandie silently prayed it was not the tenement house where she and Jonathan had been rescued from the roof. So many poor people were living there that a collapsed building could lead to a disaster.

Chapter 12 / Unexpected Visitors

Instead of taking their coats and hats to their room, Mandie and Celia threw them over their arms and rushed after Jonathan. He looked back at them and grinned. "I knew you'd follow me," he said. "I have to find Jens. Come on." He was still carrying his coat and hat.

As they came into the hallway to the kitchen, they spotted Jens hastily putting on his coat and hat and starting out the back door.

"Wait!" Jonathan called after him but he kept going. They followed Jens as he rushed toward the carriage that was still standing under the portico. They managed to jump inside the vehicle with Jens as Hodson came running to drive the carriage. Mrs. Yodkin was watching from the side door as they sped away.

"Where are you going, Jens?" Jonathan asked as the carriage swayed from the speed.

"To help with the collapsed building," Jens replied, sitting sideways and staring out the window.

The three young people looked at the butler but didn't say anything else. They were soon in the neighborhood where Jonathan and Mandie had been on the roof of the old building. And as Hodson pulled the carriage to a stop, they anxiously looked ahead.

"Jonathan, it is the tenement house we were in!" Mandie said with a loud gasp. "Oh, what can we do?"

Jens pushed open the door and jumped down to the street. "I will not be responsible for you if you leave the carriage," he told the three young people and then rushed down the street.

Jonathan immediately stepped down from the vehicle, and the girls followed. They watched to see where Jens was going, but he disappeared into the crowd.

The tenement building was standing lopsided with half its roof gone.

"Jonathan, we must go see if we can find Angelina. She lives there, you know," Mandie told him as she put her hand on his arm.

"You're right," Jonathan agreed. "Maybe we can work our way around the crowd." He led the way on the outskirts of the mob of people, gradually pushed through some of the groups of bystanders, and came out on the street near the house where a fire truck was parked along with several police vehicles.

A policeman stopped them. "You cannot go any nearer," he told them as he held out his hands.

"Please, sir, we know a little girl who lives here, and we are trying to find her," Jonathan said.

"There is no one left in the house, and all the injured have been taken to the hospital. You will not find her here. You must move back now. If the rest of the house doesn't fall by itself, we will tear it down immediately," the policeman explained. He waved them away.

As they stepped back, Jonathan said, "We've lost Jens. I don't know what to do about the carriage. If we take it and go home, he won't have a way back."

"It's not very far," Mandie said. "Why don't we just ask Hodson to drop us off real fast, and then he can come back here to watch for Jens."

"Yes, there's nothing we can do here," Celia said.

"I suppose we'll just have to go home and wait for news. Jens can tell us all about it when he comes back," Jonathan agreed reluctantly.

Hodson drove them home and then rushed back to look for Jens. The three young people went inside the Guyer house, quickly deposited their coats and hats on the hall tree, and went to the parlor.

"Has there been any word about the people in the building that collapsed, Father?" Jonathan asked as he and the girls sat down.

"Nothing," Mr. Guyer replied. "I sent Jens to check things out, but he hasn't returned yet."

The three young people looked at each other.

"Father, did you know that as soon as you and Mrs. Hamilton left last night, Jens went out?" Jonathan asked. "And he wasn't back when we went to bed about eleven o'clock."

Mr. Guyer looked at his son and replied, "Why, no, I didn't know that. Did he say where he was going?"

"Evidently no one knew where he went," Jonathan said. "I asked Mrs. Yodkin about it, and she said he just put on his coat and hat and left."

"I'll have to talk to him about that," Mr. Guyer said. He glanced at Mrs. Hamilton and added, "We have a strict rule around here now that Jonathan is staying home and going to a local school. Hodson and Jens cannot go out at the same time. One must be here at all times. And you know Hodson was driving us and of course didn't return until we did."

"That's a good rule to have," Mrs. Hamilton agreed. "But maybe he had an emergency of some kind. Surely he wouldn't just disregard your orders."

"He never has that I know of," Mr. Guyer said. "There might have been something important that came up, but he has not mentioned it to me today."

"It might have had something to do with the visitor I told you about," Jonathan suggested.

"We'll see," his father promised.

The white dog rose from the hearth and came over to look up at Jonathan and whine.

"I think I'd better take Whitey outside for a few minutes," Jonathan said, reaching for the leash on the table.

"And I need to get Snowball and take him out. He's been in our room all morning," Mandie said.

"I'll go with y'all," Celia added.

After Mandie brought Snowball downstairs, the three of them made their way through the house and into the glass room on their way outside. Luckily they were silent, because as they walked through the plants, Mandie spotted Mario standing just outside the door on the patio.

"Wait," she whispered. "Look! Mario is out there."

The others paused and looked.

"Let's sneak up on him," Jonathan said. "I'll go through the kitchen with Whitey and come out the back door over there. You girls go out this door, but give me time to get there."

Mandie and Celia waited for a minute, then made their move. Mario didn't have a chance to escape with Jonathan coming from one direction and Mandie and Celia splitting off on either side of him. He just stood there in surprise as they closed in on him.

"Now we want to talk to you," Jonathan said.

"And I have come to talk to you," Mario said, frowning at him. "Where is Angelina?"

"What do you mean, 'Where is Angelina?' How do we know? You are her uncle, and you're supposed to be taking care of her, but you let her run wild and get into all kinds of things," Jonathan told the man. "We want to ask you. Where is Angelina?"

Mario looked at him in disbelief as he glanced at the two girls. "You do not know where Angelina is?" he asked.

"We want to ask you something else, too," Jonathan said as he held to the leash on the white dog. "Why did you tie up Jens in the kitchen, and why did you run away from us?"

Mario shrugged his broad shoulders as he replied, "Jens did not give us enough money, so we tie him up and take his money from his pocket. I do not know why you chase me, so I run."

The three young people looked at each other. Mandie asked, "Why should Jens give you money? What was it for?"

Mario thought for a long moment and then replied, "Because Jens owes me money, that's why."

"For what?" Jonathan asked.

Mario shrugged his shoulders again and didn't answer.

"I saw him give you that envelope in the glass room," Mandie said. "Was there money in it?"

"Yes, but not enough," Mario insisted. "Must have more money."

"Money for what?" Jonathan asked again.

"Not your business," Mario finally replied.

"Does he owe you money for something you have done for him?" Celia asked.

Mario looked at her and smiled. "Yes, I do big thing for him," he said.

"What big thing?" Jonathan asked.

"If I tell you, Jens will not give me more money. He tell me that," Mario said with a big frown. "Now where is Angelina?"

"She is your niece. You're supposed to keep up with her," Mandie said. "She's too young to be running around New York by herself. And I think you'd better find her before something happens to her."

Mario frowned again as he said sadly, "I am afraid something bad has already happened."

"We went over to the tenement house where y'all live, and most of it is caved in. They said they are going to tear the rest of it down," Mandie told the man.

Mario looked at her and said, "Yes, I know, and I cannot find Angelina. Please tell me if you know where she has gone."

"But we don't know anything about her," Jonathan said. "My father sent Jens over there to help—"

Mario quickly interrupted, "Jens over there to help? Then I must find Jens." He turned to go.

"Wait!" Jonathan demanded, stepping closer to the man. "We want the answers to some questions. For one thing, where are Angelina's parents?"

Mario stopped and said, "Her mother was my sister and she died in Spain. I bring Angelina to United States with me."

"What about her father?" Mandie asked. "Where is he?"

Mario shrugged and said, "I cannot tell you that."

"Cannot tell me, or do not know?" Mandie asked.

The man looked puzzled with the question and merely shrugged again.

"Angelina has the same last name as Jens," Jonathan said, "and she said you and Jens were friends in Spain. My father hired Jens from an earl in England, and Jens has always said he is English. Are you related?"

Mario thought for a moment, then looked at Jonathan and said, "I am not to tell or Jens will stop giving me money."

"Tell what? Come on, Mario," Jonathan insisted. "If you don't want to tell me, I'll have my father talk to you, and he has a way of getting answers to his questions. He is a secret government agent, you know."

Mario's mouth flew open in shock. "Secret government agent?"

"Yes, he is," Mandie confirmed.

At that moment Mr. Guyer called to them from the door of the greenery. "What's taking so long?" He came out and walked up to them, squinting as he looked at Mario. "Who is this?"

Mario was practically shaking with fright. He

wouldn't look directly at Mr. Guyer.

"This man's name is Mario, Father," Jonathan began. "He has some connection with Jens, and we're trying to find out what it is."

Mr. Guyer looked at Jonathan and asked, "Connection with Jens? Is he a relative?"

"No, Father, this is the man we told you about before," Jonathan explained. "He says if he tells us whether he's related to Jens or not that Jens will stop giving him money. But we don't know what Jens gives him money for."

"Well, now, Mario, you might as well tell us the truth because you can be sure I will interrogate Jens as soon as he returns," Mr. Guyer told him.

Mario frowned and finally looked straight at Mr. Guyer. "Then I will tell you," he began. "Jens was married to my sister. My sister dies. I bring Angelina to United States, and Jens pay me money to keep her."

"Jens was married to your sister?" Mr. Guyer questioned. "Jens told me he did not have a family when I hired him in England to come here and work."

"Jens and my sister have baby, Angelina. My sister dies soon, and Jens moves back to England and leaves Angelina with me and my family in Spain," the man explained.

"And now he pays you to keep her? Why doesn't he keep her?" Mr. Guyer asked. "He has never told me a thing about this."

Mandie was listening to every word. She looked at her friends and they both nodded at her. The three of them had been suspicious of the fact that Angelina's name was Phipps, the same as Jens's.

"He say to me you would not have him work if

he had a family," Mario said. "He say do not ever tell."

"That is a ridiculous idea," Mr. Guyer said.

"I have to go now and find Angelina. She was in the tenement that fell in," Mario said.

"Yes, you go and find her. And I want you also to find Jens and bring both of them to me immediately," Mr. Guyer told the man. "Now hurry."

Mario looked at him in surprise and then smiled. "Sí, señor, I will be back." He hurried across the garden.

Mr. Guyer turned to the young people and said, "Let's go back inside now. We will be eating soon."

But soon afterward they were all sitting in the parlor when Jens appeared in the doorway and asked, "You wished to see me, sir?"

"Yes, Jens," Mr. Guyer replied as he rose from his chair and came to stand in the doorway with the man. He glanced out into the hallway and called, "Come in here, Mario. This concerns you, too."

The three young people and Mrs. Hamilton watched as Mario came to Jens's side and silently waited.

"I don't know whether Mario told you or not, but I now know the whole story about your having been married to Mario's sister and Angelina being your daughter," Mr. Guyer began. "For heavens' sakes, man, why do you not claim your own daughter? Your own flesh and blood?"

Jens shuffled his feet and finally spoke. "I have no way to take care of her, sir. Therefore I have been paying Mario to do that."

"No way to take care of her? I pay you a mighty good salary, Jens," Mr. Guyer told him firmly.

"But, sir, I have no place for her to live," Jens continued objecting.

"No place to live? That is another foolish idea," Mr. Guyer said. "You know as well as I do that I own the building next door and that there is plenty of room in there for anyone who works for me to live."

Jens dropped his eyes and didn't say anything.

"Now, Jens, I will tell you here and now, once and for all," Mr. Guyer began. "If you do not set up a home for that daughter to live with you in that building, I will have to discharge you. I have no use whatsoever for any man who doesn't take care of his family."

"Yes, sir, I understand," Jens said. Then, after a short pause, he said, "Thank you, sir. I will move over there today and bring her with me. You see, the tenement house that collapsed is the one where she lived with Mario."

"I'm terribly sorry about that," Mr. Guyer said. "Then Mario has no home, either. You will fix up the ground floor apartment for you and your daughter and then prepare a room on the second floor for Mario. I believe there's that much space vacant over there right now."

Mr. Guyer turned to Mario and said, "Mario, what kind of work do you do?"

Mario seemed shy. "I do not have job," he said. "I teach the school in Spain."

"Oh, so you're a schoolteacher," Mr. Guyer said with interest. "Then we'll see about setting up a room or two for you to tutor students in Spanish. You ought to be able to make a good living with that."

The three young people had moved closer and closer as the conversation had gone on, and now they were standing next to the three men. Mario surprised them all as he suddenly hugged each one of them, saying, "Thank you, thank you!"

"I'm so glad for you, Mario," Mandie said.

"And for Angelina," Celia added.

"But where is Angelina?" Jonathan asked.

"We have not been able to find her, Master Jonathan," Jens volunteered.

"Was she actually in the house when it collapsed?" Mr. Guyer asked.

"We don't think so, sir," Jens said. "The police had thoroughly searched the place and had taken all the injured to the hospital. I went to the hospital, but I couldn't find her there, either."

"Then you and Mario must keep looking for her," Mr. Guyer said. "You may take the carriage if you like."

"Thank you, sir," Jens said. "We shall return as quickly as possible."

"Gracias, señor," Mario said, almost bowing with his thanks.

The men left, and Mr. Guyer went back to sit by the fireplace with Mrs. Hamilton.

"That was a very kind thing you did there, Lindall," Mrs. Hamilton commented.

"In a way," he said with a grin. "I don't want to lose Jens."

The three young people sat down on the settee and discussed the events of the day.

"I hope Jens can control Angelina. She seems so wild," Jonathan remarked.

"I hope they can find her," Mandie said.

"Angelina will be awfully thrilled about living next door to the white dog, won't she?" Celia said.

"She certainly will. There's a gate in the other

wall of the garden that opens into the garden to the building where she'll be living," Jonathan told the girls. "I'll just have to make her understand that he is not to be taken out on the street."

"I'm glad she's going to have a home," Mandie said.

Mr. Guyer spoke across the room to them. "Young ladies, everything is off schedule because of the accident, but Mrs. Yodkin will be announcing dinner any minute now," he told them and then added, "I do hope you don't regret staying with us instead of at the hotel."

"I appreciate your asking us," Celia said.

"Mr. Guyer, I've enjoyed visiting here in your home," Mandie said. "You and Jonathan have just got to come visit us."

"At your house or at your grandmother's in Asheville where you go to school?" Mr. Guyer asked.

"Oh, at my house, of course, when I'm home from school," Mandie said. "However, if you're ever in Asheville when I'm there, you'll just have to come and visit at my grandmother's house."

Mr. Guyer looked hard at her and smiled faintly as he said, "Your grandmother would have to ask me first. However, perhaps we might come during Christmas week to your mother's house. We'll see."

Mandie thought of how her grandmother had tried to prevent her from coming to visit the Guyers. She couldn't think of a polite way to ask the question, but she wanted to know what was wrong between her grandmother and Mr. Guyer. She glanced at Jonathan and realized he was grinning. And even Celia was smiling.

"I'll ask my grandmother to ask you and Jonathan," Mandie said, which was the only thing she could think of to say.

At that moment Mrs. Yodkin appeared at the door to the hallway. She looked directly at Mandie and said, "Begging pardon, miss, but there's someone at the front door asking for you."

Mandie jumped up and said, "It's probably Dr. Plumbley after all."

"No, miss, this man is an Indian if I ever saw one," Mrs. Yodkin said with a frown. "There are two white people with him."

Mandie didn't wait to hear more. "Uncle Ned!" she cried, excitedly rushing for the door.

And she got another surprise when she looked out the front door. There beside Uncle Ned stood Dr. Woodard and his son, Joe, from back home in North Carolina.

"Oh, I'm so glad to see y'all!" she cried, reaching for Uncle Ned's hand. "Come on in. Everybody is in the parlor."

"Wait, Miss Amanda," Dr. Woodard told her. He turned back to the porch and motioned toward a girl who was sitting on the steps. "Does this girl live here? She was a little scratched up in the building accident and said she didn't have a place to stay but that y'all would let her come here."

"Oh, Angelina!" Mandie exclaimed as she went out onto the porch to the girl. Jonathan and Celia had followed Mandie to the door, and now they all stared at the girl. She had a small bandage around one hand, and when she looked up at them, Mandie could see that she had been crying.

"Come, Angelina," Jonathan said, quickly reaching down to take her other hand. "You are going to be living in the house next door with your father. My father said so."

"My father?" the girl asked as she stood up.

"Yes, Jens is your father, didn't you know that?" Jonathan asked her.

Angelina's eyes grew round as she said, "Nobody told me."

"We're telling you now. Come on inside," Jonathan insisted, leading her into the hallway.

As everyone appeared in the doorway to the parlor, Mr. Guyer came to greet them and introduce himself. Mrs. Hamilton had met them before, and she stood by smiling as they all got acquainted.

After everyone was seated, Mandie felt a sudden silence among the young people. Joe was staring at Jonathan, and Jonathan was surreptitiously looking at him. The two had never met before, but they had heard plenty about each other.

Jonathan looked directly at Joe, cleared his throat, and said, "So you are Joe?"

"So you are Jonathan. Mandie has told me a lot about you," Joe said.

"She has told me a lot about you, too," Jonathan replied.

Mandie, trying to make them feel at ease with each other, hurriedly asked, "Joe, how did you happen to be in New York, and with Uncle Ned?"

"We came to visit a college I had thought about attending next year," Joe explained. "And somehow Uncle Ned found out where we were staying and just came walking in today."

Uncle Ned added from across the room, "Grandmother of Papoose tell me to go see Papoose all right while I visit friend in New York."

"And we happened to be downtown when that

building collapsed," Dr. Woodard explained. "In fact, we were looking for the office of Dr. Plumbley so we could say hello. But just as we got to his door, he was called to the scene and I went along to see what I could do."

"Any serious injuries?" Mr. Guyer asked.

"Well, a few cuts and scratches but no broken bones," Dr. Woodard said. "Most of the tenants were able to get out without injury, but the police are tearing down what was left standing of the old building."

At that moment Jens appeared at the door to the hallway and said, "Begging pardon, Mr. Guyer, but I could not find—" Then he saw Angelina sitting on the rug by the hearth and playing with the white dog.

Mr. Guyer looked at him and said, "She's right here, Jens. Our friend Dr. Woodard brought her here."

Angelina stood up and stared at Jens, and he stared back at her. Then she suddenly ran across the room to him, pulled on his hand, and said, "You are my father. I want to go home with you."

Jens stood there speechless until Mr. Guyer said, "Jens, take Angelina to Mrs. Yodkin and ask her to get one of the maids to bathe her. She needs fresh clothes."

"Yes, sir, but I do not have any clothes for her," Jens said.

Mandie jumped up and said, "I'll see what I have in my things that she might be able to wear until you buy her something. I know I have a skirt that can be rolled up at the waistband to fit her."

"I'll go with you," Celia said, rising to follow.

"Just don't be too long, girls," Mrs. Hamilton

said. "We will be eating soon."

Jens took Angelina down the hallway as Mandie and Celia hurried to their room. Once inside, Mandie closed the door and leaned against it.

"I really feel strange about Joe and Jonathan finally meeting. They seem so hostile to each other," she said, taking a deep breath.

"Just think what it's going to be like when Jonathan comes to stay at your house for Christmas week. Joe will be there, too, most likely," Celia reminded her.

"I know," Mandie said as she closed her eyes and frowned. "This is going to be an interesting Christmas this year."

She wondered whether or not she should have asked Mr. Guyer and Jonathan. But it was too late now. It had been done. And they were most likely coming. And she knew the Woodards always came to her house during Christmas.

"Oh well," she said to herself, "I'll think about it when I get home."

A Special Letter to the Author

Dear Mrs. Leppard,

My mom gave me the first two Mandie books when I was eight years old. We were in the car moving to Asheville, North Carolina, and I remember looking at the books under the gas station lights and trying to read them between streetlights as we drove. As much as I loved traveling, it was always hard to say good-bye to a place that had become home. I loved reading about Mandie's adventures, and instead of thinking about how much I'd missed West Virginia, I couldn't wait to get to know Asheville.

While living there, I wrote school reports about the Cherokee Indians, admired their artwork, and learned about the area's history. I enjoyed reading about places in your books and being able to say, "I've been there!"

When I was ten my family moved from Asheville, and away from the mountains of the South entirely, to central Iowa. We had only been there two weeks when my dad died in an accident just after Christmas on the way to get a trailer load of our belongings in Asheville.

My dad had an unwavering faith in God's provision, he was cheerful, fun, and strong; he made my world secure. Like Mandie, I had to realize that

God would still take care of me, even through something as difficult as this. Like Jim Shaw, my dad was a friend to everyone he knew. In fact, the accident happened while he was trying to help a stranger who was having trouble on the highway. His gravestone has John 15:13 written out, and everyone said he died the way he lived, helping wherever he could.

When I found out about the accident, the first things I asked for—everything was still in boxes from the move—were my Mandie books. Somehow, someone found them for me, and I read them again for encouragement that I would also survive this loss. I didn't have all the adventures Mandie did, but I needed that same strength as the oldest of three children who moved across the country to two different homes, lost their dad, and started at two new schools in the space of one year. I also missed the mountains and the southern way of life. I was glad to hold on to some of that through your books as I made the transition to the Midwest, which turned out to be beautiful, too.

I'm a junior in college now, and only someone with a very good ear can hear my slight southern accent. My mom still gets me the new Mandie books. God has taken care of me, in ways no less miraculous than the ways He worked in Mandie's life, through answered prayer, His own people, and His presence and guidance every day of my life.

I always wanted to be a writer, and although I'm currently a biology/secondary education major with a minor in English, it's still my dream to write young adult fiction. I read hundreds of books growing up, and yours were some of my favorites. They're great because they're full of adventures starring a strong, but not perfect, girl with whom readers can identify. They take place in a vivid historical setting, and they proclaim the love of God. Someday if I have a daughter, I'll take her to the mountains and pass on my Mandie books for her to read. I wanted to share with you this story of how much your stories meant in my life, and tell you *thanks so much*!

Sincerely,
Mary Lindsey